Hausgeister!

HOUSEHOLD SPIRITS OF GERMAN FOLKLORE

Hausgeister!
Household Spirits of German Folklore

Published by Eye of Newt Books Inc. • www.eyeofnewtpress.com
Eye of Newt Books Inc. 56 Edith Drive, Toronto, Ontario, M4R 1C3

First edition edited & published by Brill Deutschland GmbH, Florian Schäfer,
Janin Pisarek, Hannah Gritsch: *Hausgeister*, Köln 2020;
Second edition edited & published by Eye of Newt Books Inc., Toronto 2023

ISBN: 9781777791810

Printed in China

—

Library and Archives Canada Cataloguing in Publication

Title: Hausgeister! : household spirits of German folklore / Florian
   Schäfer, Janin Pisarek, Hannah Gritsch.
Other titles: Hausgeister! English
Names: Schäfer, Florian, author. | Pisarek, Janin, author. | Gritsch, Hannah, photographer.
Description: Translation of: Hausgeister!: Fast vergessene Gestalten der deutschsprachigen Märchen-
   und Sagenwelt. | Includes bibliographical references.
Identifiers: Canadiana 20220395748 | ISBN 9781777791810 (hardcover)
Subjects: LCSH: Folklore—Germany.
Classification: LCC GR166 .S3313 2023 | DDC 398.20943—dc23

Hausgeister!

HOUSEHOLD SPIRITS OF GERMAN FOLKLORE

Translator's Note:

The kobold, wichtel, and heinzelmänner described in this book are German mythological creatures, the product of their specific geographical origins, histories, and modern cultural associations in today's German-speaking world. Other folklore traditions (especially the Anglo-Saxon and Northern European) have given rise to their own treasury of mystical beings, but while creatures such as goblins, brownies, and elves bear striking similarities to their German counterparts, although related, they are the product of separate cultural traditions that influenced each other. For that reason, I have retained the German nomenclature and offered supplementary explanations where I have deemed necessary.

Joanna Scudamore-Trezek

Contents

Introduction:

Continuing the Legacy of the Illustrated Guide to the Supernatural

This book is the most important ever published on British and Irish house spirits. "But," says the confused reader, "isn't this about German and Central European hausgeister?" Yes, it is. The fact is, though, that there is no area of the British and Irish supernatural that has been more neglected than work on house spirits. In the last half-century, only Katharine Briggs produced targeted work: and that work was not among her best writing. Then, if you want to read about British house spirits (here Ireland follows, to some extent, different rules) the parallels with the house spirits of the Germanic world are striking. The red-hats, temper tantrums, gifts of clothes . . . all of these are to be found both in Britain and across the North Sea and stretch down from the Netherlands to the Danube. If you need insights, then, into how the house spirits of Lowland Scotland or the Welsh Marches work *Hausgeister!* is the book for you. It might be written about a different territory, but the lessons, the stories, and the experiences are fundamentally the same.

As to the packaging, in 1976 the great Katharine Briggs invented a new genre: the fairy dictionary—she was 78. This supernatural bestiary (for such it was) would slowly spread around the western world. It is an efficient if necessarily limited way to describe the indescribable. But as it spread, it merged with another strand of faery writing: the illustrated guide to the supernatural world, pioneered by writers like Huygen, Froud, and Lee. Now there are shelves full of ornately illustrated paranormal guides to this or that entity. *Hausgeister!*, other authors with ambitions in this sphere should take note, is the model of how to put together a supernatural bestiary. The illustrations which are actually photographs of ornately, handcrafted sculptures are, let's be frank, strangely superb. But the writing does not fall into the trap of superficiality. There is real scholarship behind the prose. There has also been the important choice to focus on just four types of house spirits (instead of the normal four hundred) and the authors show time and time again that that these "types" are, let us say, elastic categories! We talk of books that work for both popular and academic audiences. Here is a rare volume that goes even further. With its superb visuals, it is—as I found in my own household—a treat for children and adults alike.

Dr Simon Young

Dr Simon Young is a British folklore historian based in Italy. He has written extensively on the nineteenth-century supernatural. His book *The Boggart* (from Exeter University Press) and *The Nail in the Skull and Other Victorian Urban Legends* (from Mississippi University Press) published in 2022. He is the editor of *Exeter New Approaches to Legends, Folklore and Popular Legends* and teaches history at University of Virginia's Siena Campus (CET).

Preface:

Between Art and Cultural History

KOBOLD. WICHTEL. HEINZELMÄNNCHEN.

Household spirits have had many names over the centuries. Fairy-tales and legends of German folklore were filled with strange creatures, many of whom are now forgotten, swallowed by time, or given new designations and dispositions. These colourful, sometimes amusing, but often cruel creatures once featured in song and story are reflective of customs and beliefs held by past generations.

The regional folklore and legends of many Central European countries, including Germany, now endure only in the yellowed pages of dusty book collections. Long have these been absent from the classroom, rejected as outdated ideology. Yet within these legends lie fascinating insights into the hearths and homes of old, an insight that is worthy of preservation and retelling.

Fantasy novels and films are extremely popular, and Iceland's commissary of the elves is hugely alluring and a driver of tourism. Interest in foreign legendary figures and mythical creatures remains unwavering to this day, and regularly finds an outlet in modern pop culture. Despite the continued popularity of the modern revisionists, a general awareness of the cultural background behind these traditional stories is disappearing—especially with lesser-known folklore. It is therefore time to seek out the almost forgotten creatures of Central European legends.

We three contributors have worked together to trace the paths of mythical entities in German folklore. Working with an interdisciplinary team of expert academics from a wide variety of fields, we have sought those creatures which people imagined inhabit our immediate surroundings. The contributors will also feature in this book, revealing more of their personal areas of expertise.

Those looking for cruel giants or charming fairies in this volume will leave disappointed. As the title suggests, we are on the search for spirits of the house. These creatures, mostly benevolent but sometimes capricious, haunted farmsteads and castles in German-speaking regions for generations.

We invite you to come with us on a journey through the cultural past of our homeland, searching for vestiges of household spirits in old castles and bleak farmsteads. Join us and dare to peer into even the darkest reaches of our history.

Florian Schäfer, Janin Pisarek & Hannah Gritsch

Welcome:

A Journey of Discovery into the World of Fairy Tales and Legends

"Cinderella," "Sleeping Beauty," "Rapunzel," and "Snow White" are widely known fairy tales. Since 1975, the German Fairy-Tale Route has invited visitors to discover more about these fairy-tale princesses and immerse themselves in the world of the Grimm Brothers' *Tales of Children and the Home*. From Hanau, birthplace of Jacob and Wilhelm Grimm, to the places they lived in Steinau, Marburg, Kassel, Göttingen, and on toward Bremen (of *The Bremen Town Musicians*), the route offers visitors a varied program of events which trace the footsteps of the famous brothers and their mythical heroes. They include familiar fairy tales performed on modern stages; crowns, dwarf caps, and many childhood memories set in fairy-tale houses; guided tours along fairy-tale pathways; and theatrical presentations in the staged settings of noble castles and palaces, all giving visitors the chance to encounter the Grimms and their fairy-tale princesses.

Occasionally questions arise: Was "Rapunzel" really set in the tower at Trendelburg? Did "Little Red Riding Hood" come from the Schwalm region? Were the seven dwarfs of "Snow White" miners of short stature in Bergfreiheit? These questions lead us almost directly from the fantasy world of fairy tales to the realm of legends—a world in which reality and popular belief coalesce.

Some legendary figures such as *Rübezahl* or the Pied Piper of Hamelin are as familiar as the famous fairy-tale princesses. But what about the goblins, kobolds, and moss women? For centuries, these so-called household spirits ruled the world of legends and popular belief. And this is where *Hausgeister!* comes in, as an almost perfect way of affirming and augmenting the invitation to discover the world of fairy tales and legends. The texts and images of dwarfs, fiery house dragons, and helpful elves reveal what was hidden from view—at least for the unpractised eye—tucked away in the folds of princesses' gowns, in the cracks of castle walls, in the corners of museum cabinets. They throw light into dark corners and reveal a mythical world which had seemed almost lost to memory.

May this book inspire countless readers, young and old, to start a journey of discovery in that liminal space between history and legend.

Benjamin Schäfer
Managing Director
Deutsche Märchenstraße e.V.
www.deutsche-maerchenstrasse.com/en

The Spirit Hunters

FOLLOWING THE FOOTSTEPS OF MYTHICAL CREATURES

FLORIAN SCHÄFER

Florian is the driving force behind *Forgotten Creatures*. The biologist grew up in a small village in the middle of Germany and has been fascinated by the legends and fairy tales of his homeland since childhood. In his artistic work he combines his knowledge of anatomy and ecology, as well as his in-depth knowledge of cultural science. In this way Florian creates unique creatures and spirits that give us insight into our own cultural past.

JANIN PISAREK

Janin is a folklorist and responsible for the technical quality control at *Forgotten Creatures.* She studied folklore, cultural history, and educational science at the Friedrich Schiller University in Jena, Germany. Her thesis on wolves and were-wolves in folktales, oral history and German folk belief, including the current return of the wolf, received the Special Promotion Prize from the Märchen-Stiftung Walter Kahn.

HANNAH GRITSCH

Hannah is a communication designer with a focus on photography and graphic design. With her unique style, Hannah manages to breathe life into Florian's sculptures in a fascinating way. She is the designated contact person for all graphic and aesthetic issues. She also supports the project with her experience in the advertising industry.

Chapter 1

Past and Present

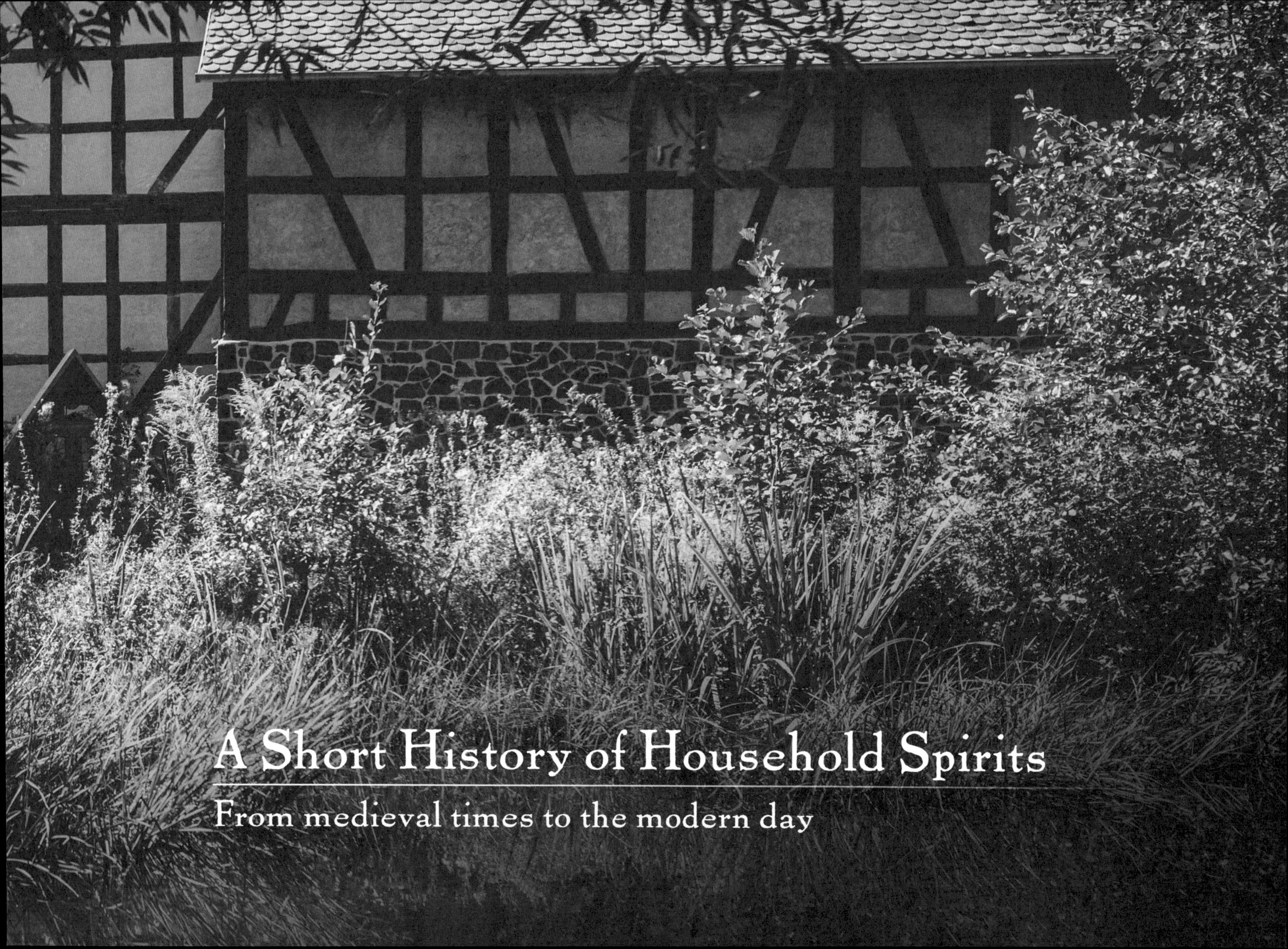

A Short History of Household Spirits

From medieval times to the modern day

EVERY ERA HAS ITS HOUSEHOLD SPIRIT

It is curious that historical sources that tell of spirits almost always follow a political or social agenda. These written sources are more than mere fantasy featuring kobolds and dwarfs but are reflections on culture and context. But, why use household spirits in this way? To answer this question, we will set off on a short journey through time, from the medieval period to the modern day. We will first have a look at the subject of household spirits in general, before turning to each creature in more detail.

Medieval period (750 – 1500)

We first come across evidence of belief in household spirits in the early medieval period. The Benedictine monk Notker Labeo (950 – 1022) clearly had a taste for philosophy and language. Today he is regarded as one of the most important translators of biblical texts. He translated various ancient texts and commented on the works of Aristotle (384 – 322 BCE). Notker believed that the origins of household spirits lay in the Roman house gods, the *penates* and *lares*. He not only tried to remain true to the original Latin in his translations, but also tried to convey the meaning behind these terms into Old High German as accurately as possible. In the tenth century he invented two terms for *lares* and *penates*:

- **ingoumo:** something that can be observed in the house, and which is treated with respect.
- **insgesid:** a fellow occupant.

These terms define something people believed in, which wasn't quite a god, was intangible, and therefore was also taboo. What was clear was the evidence of the respect shown to these unknown powers at that time. The term *kobold* first appears in thirteenth century manuscripts, before gradually replacing most of the other names in use. However, descriptions of kobolds were scarce, and so, while we know they were respected, we can say almost nothing about how people in the medieval period really perceived these creatures.

Slowly, the perception of household spirits and the customs associated with them was affected by the Church's efforts to combat superstition. The demonization of former heathen gods began with the first efforts to convert the Germanic peoples. History tells us that in 981/982 AD the Saxon bishop Friðrekur used prayer, song, and holy water to drive out the spirit *Armadr* which dwelled in a stone belonging to the Icelander Koðrán von Giljá. According to popular tradition, Koðrán then consented to be baptized.

While missionaries fought demons abroad, the faithful battled local belief in spirits within the home. In the mid-thirteenth century, Rudolf von Schlesien denounced the practice of worshipping household deities called *Stetewaldiu* as idolatry. This is remarkable because it is one of the earliest written mentions of household dieties.

Humanism—Reformation (1470 – 1600)

The *Interpretatio Christiana*, which occurred in the 1500s, was a strategy for Christianization that involved the recasting of religious and cultural activities, beliefs, and imageries. Effectively, the formerly good household spirits were recast as devious demons. Many modern versions of traditional legends reveal this demonization process which stemmed in equal measure from both the Catholic and emerging Reformed Church. This corruption of the household spirits was two-pronged: over time these supernatural figures were ascribed the defining characteristics of the Devil, while "owners of household spirits" were ostracized by their communities, vilified as being in cahoots with the Devil, and branded as witches.

WITCHES—FROM INJURIOUS SPIRIT TO WISE WOMEN

Our modern image of witches as human women with a secret knowledge of herbs and visionary powers is not supported by historical sources. In fact, the first linguistic precursors to the word *"Hexe"* sporadically appears as early as the medieval period, although at this time the term is only used to describe evil spirits. It is only in the fifteenth century that we first see Hexe ascribed to humans accused of being practitioners of sorcery. The connection between evil and sorcery lies here in lexicon and so witches became the symbol of blasphemy. One reason for this development may lie in the agrarian crisis which blighted the Late Medieval Period: long, cold winters led to crop.failure in many regions of Europe resulting in malnutrition and disease, an influx of pestilence such as rats, and sowing dissent among the peoples. Responsibility for the failed harvests was quickly attributed to minorities and marginalized groups and it is here that we find witches.

One of the most important manuscripts dating from the fifteenth century was the *Malleus Maleficarum*, a treatise on the prosecution of witches written by Heinrich Kramer (around 1430 – 1505).

The Church was primarily concerned with a witch's ability to acquire a spirit through a covenant with the Devil. By entering such a pact, a human could pay for wealth and good fortune with their souls. During this period, one religious figure stands out: Martin Luther (1483 – 1546) initiator of the Reformation. Over several decades he issued proclamations on sorcery, witches, and household spirits in his sermons, lectures, speeches, and letters. Luther was convinced that the Devil was actively seeking to tempt humans and he believed in the Devil's Pact and advocated the legal persecution of sorcerers and witches. Luther's speeches from *Table Talk*, first published in 1566, make plain his thoughts on demons, devils, and witches. He thought demonizing spiritual beings was an insufficiently radical approach. Des-

pite this, he believed these beings were largely harmless, and the ever-lurking Devil impotent in the face of the overriding power of God. Although the Protestant and Roman Catholic Churches engaged intensively in the eradication of demons, they did not entirely succeed in conflating the tradition of household spirits with being rooted in the Devil.

Preoccupation with the phenomenon of household spirits reached beyond the Church as well. Count Froben Christoph von Zimmern (1519 – 1566) saw spirits as fallen angels which, once on earth, transformed into *Erdmännlein*, or dwarfs. It was his belief that they took on a physical form and sought out human company in the hope that performing good deeds would lead to forgiveness. Count von Zimmern also turned to Roman terminology, dividing the spirit world into good spirits, the *lares familiares*, and evil creatures, the *lares domestici*. This view countered Christian teaching because there lingered a latent belief in household spirits, though in his view household spirits were fallen angels. He recorded his views in texts including the *Zimmern Chronicle* which are today regarded as an outstanding source on the culture of sixteenth century nobility. Additionally, the Swiss physician and natural philosopher, Theophrastus Bombast von Hohenheim (1493/94 – 1541), today known as Paracelsus, spoke out vehemently against condemning spirits as demons, instead arguing that these elemental spirits were part of God's creation and therefore natural. In his *A Book on Nymphs, Sylphs, Pygmies, and Salamanders, and on the Other Spirits* he explained his theory of the connection between elemental spirits and the natural world, and within that text he mentions the activity of household spirits.

However, as the *Interpretatio Christiana* became increasingly established, these human-like or elemental creatures without souls turned into incarnations of the Devil, frequently casting spells over people by means of lascivious enticements and debauched temptations. Acceptance of these Christian intrusions into popular belief was limited and so several of these figures withstood Christian attempts to demonize them and retained their pagan identities.

Baroque (1600 – 1720)

During the Baroque period's interdisciplinary approach to scholarship, permitted topics of academic discussion included sorcery, ghostly appearances, and Satanism. This was mirrored by a growing resistance to witch trials and exorcism. Scholars examining the world of household spirits found a diverse range of explanations for these creatures. There was also a growing divergence between views of spirits as manifestations of the Devil and a perception of spirits as supernatural beings and spirits of the dead. Various scholars adopted the terms "*lares domestici*" and "*lares familiares,*" with the latter increasingly being applied to a different creature: the "*spiritus familiaris,*" a form of devilish genie.

The publication of popular science collections in a variety of scientific fields—the precursor to the encyclopedia—was particularly in vogue during this period, especially in German literature. One of the most famous authors of the time was Magister Johannes Praetorius (1630 – 1680) who published more than 50 books and was known for his compilations of fairy tales and curious legends. Today he is best remembered for his collection of legends about the Rübezahl, a folkloric mountain spirit of the Krkonoše Mountains. In his 1666 *Eine Neue Weltbeschreibung* (description of the New World), Praetorius details wondrous creatures over hundreds of pages: he reports on child dragons and men of fire; kobolds and mandrakes; werewolves; forest dwellers; and wind people.

It is usually kept in a small, tightly sealed bottle, appearing not quite like a spider, not quite like a scorpion, but constantly moving. It remains in the pocket of the person who buys it; he may put the small bottle down wherever he will, it always returns to him, wherever he is. It brings great luck, reveals hidden treasures, makes its owner popular, but feared by their enemies and as strong as steel and iron in battle, so that its owner is always victorious, and protects him from arrest and prison.

But whoever keeps it until their death must join it in Hell, which is why the owner seeks to sell it. But it can only be sold for less than it was bought, so that it ends up with he who has paid with the smallest coin. "

Grimm, Jacob & Wilhelm. *Deutsche Sagen*, (Munich: 1965), p. 137.

The Enlightenment (1720 – 1785)

From the eighteenth century onwards, scientific thought underwent a process of demythologizing the supernatural world. The Enlightenment battled against the metaphysical-demonological teachings of the previous century and so the belief in supernatural creatures disappeared, and with it the belief in household spirits. There arose a desire to provide a rational and scientific explanation for the phenomenon of nature and the house that was physical and rational.

In his work *Physicalisch- und Historisch-Erörterte Curiositæten*, the physician Johann Jacob Bräuner (1737) argued against the belief in miracles. Bräuner sought natural explanations for the noises in houses allegedly caused by spirits. Another champion of this demythologizing process was Elias Caspar Reichard (1714 – 1791): this German educator and author took a detailed and particularly critical view of popular belief and magic:

"This mad delusion is particularly deeply embedded amongst the mob in Thüringen. If one looks at these people carefully, one sees simple-minded and ignorant women, largely old women and young mothers, who believe the same things that other equally mad hags have told them [. . .] When found in men, they are indisputably only those who have been told such nonsense during their childhoods by their superstitious aunts and carers, and who have either not had the opportunity of teaching by sensible people, or of reading the texts which were sent to erase this foolish idea; or are those who lacked the necessary ability and steadfastness needed to apply the more proper views and understanding they learned at the right time in their lives."

Elias Caspar Reichard, *Vermischte Beiträge einer nähern Einsicht in das gesammte Geisterreich*, (Helmstedt: 1781).

Here Reichard represents the views of educated males on what they felt to be the backward population; his words demonstrate what would now be seen as the latent classism and sexism of the late-eighteenth century. He assigned the belief in spirits to the unthinking acceptance of hearsay and a lax upbringing that relies on generations of women. Belief in these beings was quickly degraded and devalued as the superstitions of an uneducated populace; people who believed in spirits were deemed to be stupid, simple-minded, and fearful.

Romanticism and industrialization (From 1800)

By the nineteenth century, probably only very few people still believed in the beings which populated the legends and fairy tales told around the hearth. The rise of industrialization imposed social upheaval, with urbanization and rural depopulation as a result. Romanticism was the response during this period, an attempt to return to (supposedly) original values: in their works, writers and artists created partly fantastical worlds, invoking a non-existent past and a lost harmony with the natural world. The medieval period, especially, was glamorized as an ideal. In an increasingly industrialized and technical world, the things and places that for centuries had generated fear in people became idyllic. Magic was once again welcome in the world.

This was the period in which collections of folk poetry first began to be compiled. The brothers Jacob (1785 – 1863) and Wilhelm (1786 – 1859) Grimm acquired world fame with their *Tales of Children and the Home*. Interestingly, it was not the "common people" that the brothers questioned when compiling their collection, but middle-class women from the Hessian nobility. In the spirit of the Romantic period, the Grimms wished their collection to create the impression of tales originating from folklore and collectively handed down. In his book on German mythology, Jacob Grimm attempted to reconstruct the mythology of the Germanic peoples through the medium of legends, fairy tales, and customs.

"Every legend is based in myth [. . .] where distant events have been lost in the darkness of time, there they merge with legends, providing sustenance, and where the myth has been weakened and is in danger of being lost, there history is a support."

Jacob Grimm, *Deutsche Mythologie*, (Wiesbaden: 1992).

Jacob Grimm saw in the legends "a distant echo of old Germanic mythology," thereby following the mythological school which grew from the Romantic movement. The idea that household spirits and spirits of the natural world were old Germanic gods renewed and repackaged was uncritically accepted until the late twentieth century. Today's folklore and narrative research has overcome this mythological interpretation. There is no historical evidence that clearly supports a connection between old German gods and the beings from newer legends and fairy tales. Yet in some way these ideas have survived to the current day, especially in neo-Pagan circles and fantasy novels (i.e., *American Gods* by Neil Gaiman, 2001).

As well as the Brothers Grimm, two other collectors are worthy of note: today writer and pharmacist Ludwig Bechstein (1801 – 1860) from Thüringen is primarily known for his published collection of German folktales. Bechstein's *Deutsches Sagenbuch* (1853), a comprehensive collection of German legends, was not as popular as his collection of German fairy tales but is still referenced as a valuable source on German folklore.

Like the Grimms, Bechstein was also a politically active partisan, as evidenced in his lyrics and prose. He made many changes to his collections of legends and fairy tales. Like the Grimms, he was a proponent of national values which he strove to underpin with a mythology designed to encourage a sense of community. Although these collectors' literary works were criticized almost immediately after their publication, the Brothers Grimm and Bechstein presented themselves as chroniclers of literary tales, rather than their authors.

The third person in this series of collectors of folk legends is the folklorist Franz Xaver Schönwerth (1810 – 1886) whose texts were long ignored. Between 1852 and 1886 he researched the life of the population of Bavaria's Upper Palatinate district. He published a small part of his extensive research between 1857 and 1859 in *Sitten und Sagen aus der Oberpfalz Erstdruck*, his three-volume publication on customs and legends from the region. In contrast to the Grimms, he largely focused on the ordinary lives of the rural, common people, describing their daily lives and customs.

Thus, the major collections of legends published in the nineteenth and twentieth centuries reflected the need to both preserve and above all encourage an element of German—and thus national—identity. Stories were collected, altered, and then adapted to suit the writer's agenda.

Throughout our history, household spirits have served as gods, bogeymen, scapegoats, and as the embodiment of our desires and fears. Historical report, oral tales, and written legends clearly show that these creatures are not rigid constructs, but instead fluid personas that mutate in response to cultural context. These creatures blur and shift in their presence in the songs, amusing tales, and especially the legends of the last two centuries. Today these legends are a treasury and, together with a few other sources, form the basis for the work in this book, as will be seen throughout the following pages.

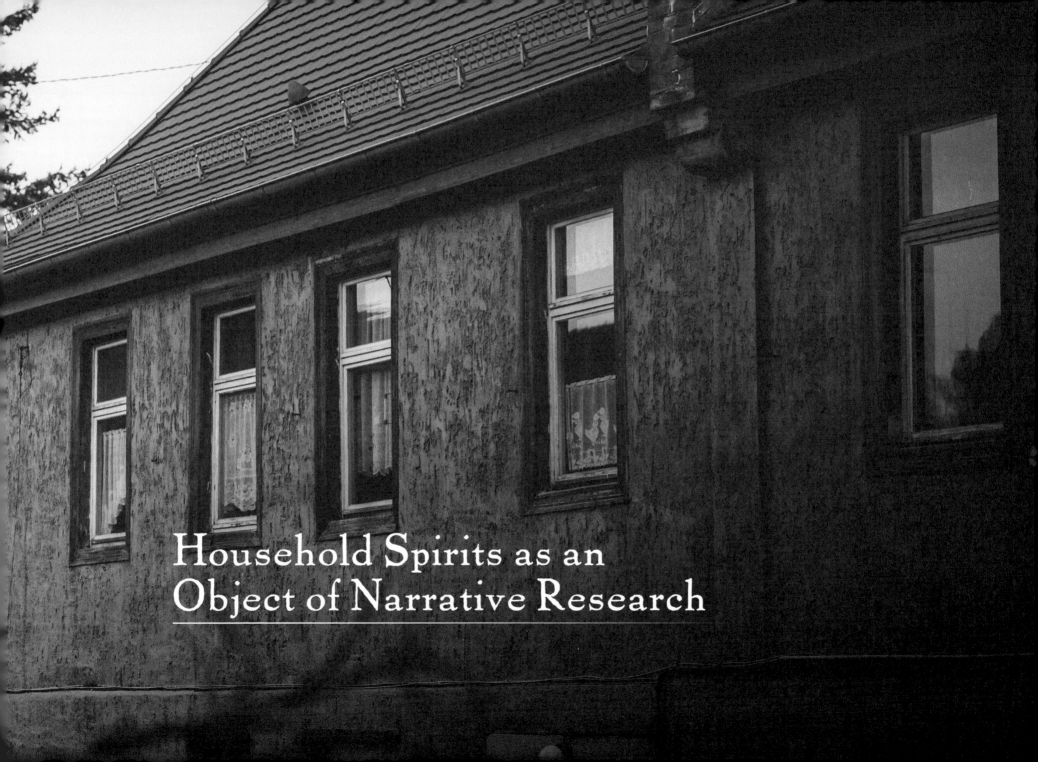

Household Spirits as an
Object of Narrative Research

ON DEMONOLOGICAL LEGENDS IN A RURAL MILIEU

Household spirits and other supernatural beings are mainly found in the world of German folktales. Confusion can arise with the German classifications of these tales, especially when comparing German and English terms: In German, the term *"Sage"* (Engl: "legend") refers to a folk story that often arises from people themselves and is (initially) transmitted orally. In contrast to the fictitious *"Märchen"* (Engl: "fairy tale"), Sage refers to real and specific places and people or relates true events. The German term *"Legende,"* on the other hand, describes a didactic, popular story from the life of a saint, in which the truth at the core of the tale is usually embellished in an imaginative manner. In the following, we will use the English terms (legend for Sage and fairy tale for Märchen).

A legend is associated with a place, a time, and a specific person, giving the impression of having been an actual historical event. Legends have their own perception of the real world, one which reflects the collective wisdom of the people. This is particularly clear in historical legends, which focus on an actual past event or person. Legends which explain the origin of various objects and phenomena, such as an unusual rock formation, a particular animal's characteristic, or an unusual family name, are etiological legends.

WHAT ARE DEMONS?

Originally, a demon was a supernatural being found in folk tales, assigned an intermediate position between gods and people, and equipped with healing or harmful powers. Once a neutral term, under the influence of Christianity and following rise of the *Interpretatio Christiana*, demons became associated with the Devil, mutating into a symbol of evil. Luther, for example, regarded kobolds (which shall be discussed in their own section on page 31) serving in the monastery as the Devil himself. Today the term "demon" is generally understood as an evil creature, bringing harm to those around it.

Mythological or demonological legends often centred around a supernatural encounter which could bring either salvation or damnation to either or both the human and supernatural creature. This narrative form is characterized by its mythical elements, supernatural creatures, or people who use magical powers. They tell of encounters with the "*Wilde Jagd*" (or "Wild Hunt"), witches and druids, ghostly phenomena and poltergeists, nightmares, or household spirits—manifestations that we would today classify as psychological or parapsychological phenomena. They include legends of the Devil, dwarf legends, and ancestor legends, and each of these types of legends has its own subcategories. They all share the motif of the supernatural invading the human world, or vice versa, and involve situations of conflict. They also evidence a belief in a world filled with the supernatural, and more specifically demons.

This intrusion of the supernatural into human lives and cultural landscapes frequently leads to a clash of conflicting religious beliefs, provocations, and violations of taboo. The tale generally goes as follows: the supernatural and human meet in a tense situation or conflict and the relationship can be regulated by a form of contract based on exchange, aid, service, and cooperation, but usually ends in disaster. As these confrontations constitute the central element in this type of legend, they are equally about human actions and behaviour. Indeed, humans are usually faced with the consequences of violating a social norm. Humans must adapt, fulfill conditions, or demonstrate humility to come out of the encounter unharmed, even rewarded. The legends that show the action and reaction of the household spirits, allow for a reflection on what was considered socially acceptable at the time and over time, as the legend itself is remoulded and retold.

The demonological legend in both German folklore and narrative research has many functions. Aside from entertainment, it also has a didactic aspect in the way it portrays, moralizes, explains, or channels angst. It imparts a sense of empathy, it warns against violating taboos and social norms, and it may also explain mysterious or even impossible occurrences as a way of deflating or inflating fear of a particular phenomenon, object, or action. The supernatural beings effectively function as "rectifiers" of human misconduct. In this sense, these legends are examples of successful and unsuccessful solutions to existential conflicts.

The world of German legends associated with the rural populace is particularly full of these supernatural beings—this is likely because of their dependence on nature. Mainly farmers and farming communities, they would have been highly affected by the seasons, the passage of the year, and natural catastrophes. This dependence on the natural world is expressed (and explained) through cohabitation with demonic beings in human or animal form. Consequently, the belief in household spirits expresses rural communities' longing for security, their striving for a form of communal life, work regulated by social norms and a structural hierarchy, as well as the possibility of the pursuit of happiness. Household spirits take on the role of supernatural law enforcers in this construct, serving as omnipresent, often patriarchal, representatives in the household.

The abundance of different anthropomorphic and zoomorphic supernatural beings throughout Central Europe appears inexhaustible; however, each of these beings often differs from another in name only. The wealth of legendary figures contrasts with a paucity of figure types and roles. According to the narrative researcher Lutz Röhrich (1922 – 2006), in terms of folklore and psychology, it is particularly interesting that the plethora of legendary figures can be reduced to the explication of relatively few basic phenomena.

All these tales of household spirits have fundamental narrative elements, or *narratemes,* and an immutable underlying structure. Their diversity is the result of drawing on local idiosyncrasies, regional variations, or blending narratives and supplementing them with figures from other folktales. This makes household spirits difficult to research as their essence is often extremely difficult to distill and their names are frequently assigned to subsequent, secondary traditions. A purely phenomenological classification, according to appearance and behaviour, would fall short of the mark as the key consideration for the relevance of these tales lies in the interaction between the human and supernatural.

Supernatural beings of legend are usually solitary figures, and particularly so in the case of household spirits, for "Every house has its [own] household spirit." They only appear collectively in groups or as families of demons in genealogical links with dwarfs and other earth spirits, especially in Northern European traditions.

It should not be forgotten that the world of the farming population was associated with another form of dependency, namely on religious and secular rulers. These legends stress ownership structures where unjustified or unearned enrichment is severely punished.

"The hütchen *lived in* Hörselberg. *They were useful to the people as helpful house-hold spirits. Where they kept watch in the stable, the cattle flourished. One of these small creatures brought prosperity to a peasant in* Hastrungfeld. *But the peasant was rude and coarse mannered and failed to appreciate this help. One day he saw the small spirit working hard to drag a straw up the stairs in the barn. Believing this was completely pointless work, he shouted at the* hütchen, *calling him a lazy rascal. The little* hütchen *immediately vanished. In place of the straw stood a large, heavy sack of grain. The farmer understood that he had been wrong to complain. But this realization brought no relief. From this point onwards he was forced to do all the work in his stable and barn himself. The blessing of having a hard worker was over. Over time he became impoverished and was reduced to begging in old age."*

Dietrich Kühn, *Sagen und Legenden aus Thüringen*, (Wartburg: 1989).

In no other area was the violation of rules and taboos so ferociously prosecuted as in the world of work—which at that time meant in service for noble landlords. Christa Bürger (*1935), a German Studies scholar, notes that a whole series of legends related to farmers tended toward didacticism and this was manifest in violations of norms being prosecuted by strong supernatural powers. In this relatively harmless example of the hütchen in Hörselberg, we see how a farmer is punished for his unjustified and coarse behaviour.

Household spirits—between popular belief and folktale
The belief in household spirits is a widespread phenomenon. Household spirits are impressive yet difficult figures to interpret. Their activities were focused on the house and farm, which could include one or more buildings, with the dual arrangement of family and livestock under a single roof, as was common from the fourteenth century onwards. They appeared in many guises, furnished with a range of different attributes, characteristics, and appearances, and took on a multitude of functions, from helpful companion to antagonistic bugbear, or neutral plant spirit. They were usually humanoid but sometimes appeared as animals or objects.

What the spirits all have in common is their recurrent, close, sometimes even erotic relationships with humans. Association with supernatural beings is seen as particularly fortunate as they bring an abundance of material wealth. However, these relationships are normally short, with the human partner usually violating a taboo such as calling the being by name, seeking out its hiding place, or failing to appreciate its

Theodor Hosemann, *Die Heinzelmännchen*, 1870, in *Illustrierte Welt* (Stuttgart), 23.

work. In the milder versions, as in the example above, the household spirit leaves the human who consequently suffers a loss of prosperity or protection.

Household spirits appear in many different forms, with many different names. Some may display marked similarities, others are more divergent, with the legends often describing their appearance, their shape, their dominant activity, and the locations in which they were active. They may have human first names or nicknames when in relationships of trust, although despite this personalization, a certain distance to humans always remains.

Despite their heterogeneity, spirits of the house are almost always protective in function. They live and work in inhabited and managed households, either as the building's occupying spirit, or as the spirit of a particularly important ancestor (often the one who built the house). In accordance with archaic beliefs, a household spirit searches out the place in which it wishes to reside. It may either arrive during the construction of the house, or later, perhaps hidden in a bundle of wood carried into the home. Some legends also suggest that household spirits could be bought. This aspect becomes important in the wake of Christianization, particularly during the later Reformation, with household spirits entering the narrative as demons with devilish intentions. In the house itself they usually have their own spirit places, or spaces in which they dwell, where humans may not disturb them. This often includes the kitchen with its stove, the barn, the stable, or the attic.

These benefits, however, could only be enjoyed by human hosts who behaved in a moral fashion and worked hard. They could not break taboos or enjoy vices such as noisiness, cursing, excessive drinking, playing cards late into the night, laziness, negligence, sexual licentiousness, refusing charity, insulting the dead, and curiosity. For as long as human behaviour was acceptable, and the trusting, sociable, and occasionally jovial contact with humans was not abused, the household spirits would dedicate all their supernatural abilities and practical skills to the service of the humans in the house. In turn, they demanded to be treated with respect and fed regularly by a preferred member of the family or household. There was an expectation of respect, that the humans would not search out the spirits themselves or their hiding places, and that they would be addressed and treated appropriately. Revenge was exacted for both deliberate and unintended taboo violations, in the form of scuffling, causing a din, physical attacks on humans and animals, contamination of food, discontinuation of the household spirit's services, their departure, or even the destruction of the house. From this point onwards, the spirits would be capricious in their dealings with humans, appearing as pests or disappearing entirely, to punish

them for their behaviour. Legend shows that this frequently led to their human host's complete impoverishment and misfortune.

It was this ambivalence that also gave rise to the desire to be rid of even the most beneficial household spirits—although this was a difficult, and at times a near-impossible endeavour. Although a household spirit's departure was often caused unintentionally, they could be actively driven away. The difficulty in driving them away, however, lay in the potential retribution from the household spirit, where improper behaviour or the violation of a taboo might encourage a household spirit to leave—it might also incur further sanctions. Household spirits could be banned from the house or driven out by a pure spirit. In some cases, a payoff in accordance with rural laws on terminating employment or a well-meant gift of clothing—which first appears in late medieval legends—was believed to help get rid of spirits. According to German narrative research, the afflicted even went so far as to tear down their

Gustave Dore, *Kobold on the stove*, 1862, in *La Mythologie du Rhine* (Boniface).

houses and rebuild them. However, it is said that *kobold geht mit dir* or "the kobold goes with you," so that this act of destruction did nothing other than cost time, resources, and money, not to mention the extra work! This clearly demonstrates the ancestral nature of the kobold as a spirit of the family, not of the house.

Tales of kobolds playing mischievous tricks, such as stealing the blanket from late risers or pulling them by the nose, are typical of more recent traditions, and reflect a temporal distance from the archaic belief in household spirits. Though these more contemporary actions are relatively harmless, they remain a reflection of the morally regulated nature of everyday life. There has been little recent research into household spirits. In a classification of legends drawn up by a special commission of experts in legends in the 1960s, no separate subcategory was assigned to household spirits. Instead, they were filed under death and the dead, haunted places and apparitions, ghosts of cultural sites, and as demons of illness or treasure, depending on their function.

In a Finnish classification dating to the 1930s which sorted legends into fifteen main groups to reflect their supernatural content, household spirits were assigned to the following categories: ghostly apparitions, death and the dead, taboo, and enhancers of prosperity. Household spirits were also often named in the context of natural or earth spirits. Compared to other legendary figures and forms, there is an astoundingly dense volume of secondary literature on household spirits—another reason for considering some of these beings in more detail . . .

Fritz Quidenus, *Bilmesschnieder*, 1908 in *Von deutscher Sitt' und Art*
(München: M. Kellerer), p.147.

Chapter 2

Household Spirits

The Kobold

" In some places almost every farmer, wife, son, or daughter has a kobold doing housework, carrying water in the kitchen, chopping wood, bringing beer, cooking, grooming the horses, mucking out the stable, and the like. Where there are kobolds at work, the cattle put on weight, and everything flourishes and succeeds. Even today we say of a maid who finishes her work quickly, 'she has the kobold.' But anyone who enrages a kobold better watch out. "

Grimm, Jacob & Wilhelm. *Deutsche Sagen*, (Munich: 1965).

Rulers of Hearth and Home

In German-speaking regions, there are more stories, tales, and legends about kobolds than any other household spirit. While a plethora of sources is on the one hand a wonderful resource, it also becomes quite difficult to reach a conclusive and consistent image of what a kobold is, what it might look like, and what its main function might be. As with all household spirits, the kobold's origins cannot be completely documented without gaps, nor is there seamless continuity between the original, supposed veneration of house gods, and today's concept of kobolds.

A PATRON SAINT WITH MANY NAMES

"What are known in old Prussian lands as Barstukken are the kobolds of North-western and Southern Germany. They have been given many and various names [. . .] Their duties are the same almost everywhere: working in the house and kitchen, cleaning floors, cellars, and stables, their reward a bowl of food or milk."

Ludwig Bechstein, *Deutsches Sagenbuch*, (Leipzig: 1853).

We find the narrative of the kobold as presiding household spirit in a spectrum of slightly altered or adapted forms. In general, though, they are the hidden rulers of the home, protectors of their houses and families. They are always solitary figures, bound closely to their house and the humans living in it. They may either be invisible or appear in many forms both animate and inanimate. The most common kobold in folktales are not abstract, numinous powers but rather a tangible or present spirit that is directly, or tangentially familial.

The first written record of the German term "kobold" dates to the thirteenth century. It is derived from the German nouns *Kob,* "house," and *Bold,* "ruler." Thus, kobolds are the rulers of house and farm. The term "kobold" replaced older names, such as the thirteenth century *Stetewalden* which translates as "*Walter des Platzes,*" or "ruler of the place" and referred to house gods. Today kobold is the generic term, because over the centuries the idea of a kobold has not only taken on many and various forms, but it has also developed many regional names. This variety is characteristic of the tradition of German household spirits.

This abundance of names can also be misleading: in some places a *Schrazel* or *Schrat* is a wood spirit, in others a kobold. Some hütchen are kobolds, others are gnome-type spirits. Even the term "*heinzelmann*" is now applied to spirits of the kobold type.

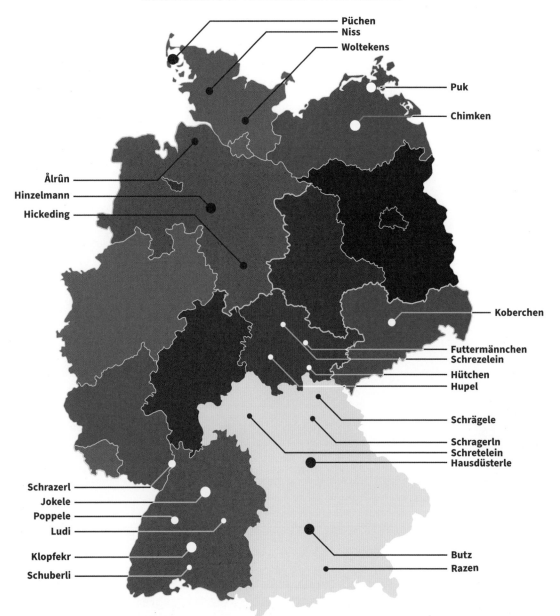

NAME VARIANTS OF THE KOBOLD WITHIN GERMANY

Püchen
Niss
Woltekens
Puk
Chimken
Ålrûn
Hinzelmann
Hickeding
Koberchen
Futtermännchen
Schrezelein
Hütchen
Hupel
Schrägele
Schragerln
Schretelein
Hausdüsterle
Schrazerl
Jokele
Poppele
Ludi
Klopfekr
Schuberli
Butz
Razen

Names were constantly subject to change; they were used, adapted, and combined, as was the idea of a household spirit itself. In Germany's eastern regions in particular, the concept of a kobold merged with that of a house dragon, and sometimes also with the *Geldmännlein*, or little money man. Consequently, as with many spirit beings, it is almost impossible to offer a description of a household spirit based purely on its name because the description doesn't always match. However, they are easier to identify when their activities, descriptions of their origins, and their sociological functions in folk belief are considered.

Many narrative researchers see the kobold as the true household spirit. In contrast to many other spirits in the house, the kobold does not leave the house and is more tightly bound to the family than any other spirit. Furthermore, we rely on a rich treasury of legends and tales which describe the kobold's actions in detail.

In 1987, the narrative researcher Erika Lindig (*1954) dedicated a complete book to the kobold, calling it *Hausgeist* because kobolds are the spirits of the household whereas other spirits in this collection come and go. She examined 106 printed collections of German folktales in 139 volumes, dating from the nineteenth and twentieth centuries, and compiled information about the kobold drawn from all German-speaking regions. She extracted no fewer than 488 unique instances of textual evidence of kobolds.

She was followed in 1995 by Dagmar Linhart. The numerous cross-references included in her comprehensive description of the household spirits of Franconian folk belief established a consistent portrayal of the belief in household spirits in German-speaking regions, and especially of the kobold.

A QUESTION OF ORIGIN—FROM RESTLESS SOULS TO TREE SPIRITS CARRIED INTO THE HOUSE

In the legends and tales of popular German belief, the kobold is usually thought to have its origins in ancestor cults. Kobolds are often ancestors, or the original builder or resident of a house, or restless souls (of children) seeking salvation through service to the family. Kobolds function as protectors of the family, and this familial connection makes it impossible for their hosts to withdraw from the relationship. The motif of "the kobold goes with you" indicates this connection.

"They believe they are seeing real people, in the shape of young children, dressed in a colourful skirt. Some have knives plunged into their backs, others are disfigured in other unpleasant ways according to the instrument used in their premature death, because they believed them to be the souls of those previously murdered in the house."

Grimm, Jacob & Wilhelm. *Deutsche Sagen,* (Munich: p.1965).

For the kobolds whose origins lie in ancestry, they do not reveal themselves and remain invisible. The potential consequences of curiosity and the overwhelming urge to see the spirit were described by the scholar Johannes Praetorius as early as 1666 in his *Eine Neue Weltbeschreibung*. The Brothers Grimm reproduce Praetorius's statements in a form more easily understood today:

"At times a maid lusts for the chance to see her little servant [. . .) as she calls the kobold, and when she refuses to stop, the spirit names the place where she should come to see him, while advising her to bring a bucket of cold water. When she arrives, she sees him lying on a cushion, naked, a large butcher's cleaver plunged into his back. Sometimes the maid is so shocked that she faints, at which point the kobold jumps up, and throws the cold water over her to revive her. Afterwards, her desire to see the kobold is gone."

Grimm, Jacob & Wilhelm. *Deutsche Sagen,* (Munich: 1965).

As well as the prevailing beliefs of the ancestor cults, a kobold could sometimes be the spirit of a place or of the earth that became a household spirit when a house was built over their dwelling. This motif is reflected in the term "*Stetewalden*," meaning *Walter des Platzes/der Ortstätte* or "ruler of the place." Indeed, according to legend some spirits could become kobolds irrespective of whether they were plant spirits or if they were—usually inadvertently—borne into the house in an

object. The legends offer many variations of the motif of carrying a spirit into the house, whether as the result of felling a tree and bringing in the logs or buying a chest of drawers containing a nature spirit which is then brought into the house.

"At the start of this century, a farmer from Baumerlenbach zu Neustadt an der Linde *purchased a locked chest of drawers, the key to which had been lost. Once he had transported the chest to his house and started to unload it, he discovered it had become very heavy. In his joy at having bought a full chest rather than an empty one, he had a blacksmith break open the lock. A little black man jumped out and disappeared behind the stove. All efforts to drive it out were in vain; as it had been carried into the house, no one could then carry it back out."*

Bernhard Baader, *Volkssagen aus dem Lande Baden und den angrenzenden Gegenden.* Vol. 1, (Karlsruhe: 1851), p. 237f.

A spirit's original nature sometimes influences their purpose or role, for instance a spirit carried into the house in a bundle of straw or brushwood becomes a household spirit whose primary role was to help during harvest. There are few tales reporting the sale of kobolds, with ownership transferred on purchase, and these tales bear many similarities to those of the geldmännlein, or little money man.

From today's perspective, what is curious about the kobold is that sometimes it has heavenly origins: in a few tales they are fallen angels who transform into kobolds to reclaim their heavenly status by doing good deeds. In the sixteenth century, an invisible spirit with the voice of a bird appeared in a castle belonging to the lords of *Sachsenheim*. When it first made itself visible, according to the *Zimmern Chronicle*, the creature appeared in the form of a fallen angel:

"It stayed with them for several years, called itself Entenwigk, *spoke, but only with the voice of a bird, indicated it was an angel fallen from heaven, but had not sinned as much as others, and so hoped to return to grace, and not to be lost forever. Sometimes it would not say how long it would need before being accepted back into heaven, at other times it indicated that it would have to wait more than a thousand years."*

Froben Christoph Zimmern, Zimmern Chronicle. Vol. 3, (Freiburg: 1881) p. 6.

As previously mentioned, Christianization heralded the demonization of household spirits and the perception of a kobold as the embodiment of the Devil. The origin of household spirits has always been a cause for discussion and scientific debate. Today it is no longer possible to determine which of these many roots is historically the oldest, and therefore the origin of the household spirit remains a mystery.

Louis Herbert Gray, "Djadek" (an ancestral spirit with the function of a household spirit [reproduction of finds from Silesia]), *Mythology of All Races* (Boston: Marshall Jones Company, 1916), p.244-245.

THE THREE FACES OF THE KOBOLD

In some ways, the origin of the word kobold contrasts with the household spirit's appearance in nineteenth and twentieth–century collections of legends: the kobold in its archaic role as a protective spirit watching over a house and the family living in it may have quickly faded, to become a poltergeist.

The oldest known kobold names, such as *ingoumo, ingesid,* and *Stetewalden*, suggest that these beings engendered a sense of awe. Archaeological findings also indicate that early humans venerated a "house spirit," treating it with respect and honouring it with sacrifices. Although it sounds plausible, in the absence of reliable sources, this explanation is only speculation.

As we have already seen, from the thirteenth century onwards the term "kobold" replaced many of the previous names used, becoming a generic term for many of the spirits active in the household. During the medieval period, three specific kobold characteristics emerged, each continuing into the nineteenth century with astounding consistency: the kobold as a protective spirit; as a teasing poltergeist; and as a mischievous devil.

The protective spirit

Earlier texts from the medieval times place the kobold in a courtly setting, or in a monastery; in more recent accounts the kobold is found in rural areas, serving both farmers and craftsmen. Here kobolds performed their original duties as guardians, traditionally serving their families, right up until the nineteenth century.

The *Petermännchen* ("Little Peter"), legends of whom date back to at least the early eighteenth century, is an example of the earlier representation of kobolds as protective spirits; he was active in Schwerin Castle. Also known as *Klopferle*, he fended off intruders, defied political opponents, was the guardian of the treasury, and protector of servants. He even tested soldiers' honesty and loyalty.

"Petermännchen once saw how a soldier, on guard in the Count's quarters, was looking at all the treasures around him. Wanting to test the soldier, he suddenly appeared before him in the room, and told the soldier to pocket some of the trinkets. The soldier refused; when Petermännchen heard this, he asked the soldier to help him once his duty was over. There would be no danger, but plenty of spoils. The soldier agreed. Once off duty, Petermännchen led the soldier through a variety of underground passages and rooms which he opened using the keys on his belt. Finally, they entered a room in which Petermännchen asked the soldier to clean all the spots of rust off his sword. The soldier succeeded apart from one last small spot; just as he was about to clean this away, a huge clap of thunder sounded, and the soldier fainted. When he came 'round, he found himself outside the gate of the castle. He felt something heavy in his bag; it was three bars of gold which, once his service was over, he used to buy himself a beautiful farm. It was only shortly before his death that he told his family how he had acquired the money."

Karl Bartsch, *Sagen, Märchen und Gebräuche aus Meklenburg 1–2*, (Vienna: 1879) p. 70-71.

We even have contemporary images of the Petermännchen: an 1823 etching by Louis Fischer of the household spirit, and a Petermännchen statue, sculpted in 1856, which decorates the facade of Schwerin Castle to this day.

Louis Fischer, *Petermännchen, the castle ghost of Schwerin*, etching/portrait, 1823, in *Mechlenbugische Sagen* (Rostock: Diigitalisierte Drucke), MK-812.c.

As described in the previous chapter, early kobolds were closely bound to the fate of a house and its inhabitants. The quiet and caring ruler of their household, representing order and morality in the house. However, this benevolence was usually withdrawn if they suffered an injustice or a breach of taboo. The guilty and lazy were regularly punished as is typical of demonological legends:

"In Thiemendorf, near Leutenberg, lived a little kobold that looked after the cattle: it zealously guarded the cattle at night, cleaned them, groomed them, chopped straw for them to lie on, so that the cattle flourished, and they shined with such health that it was a pleasure to look at the farmer's oxen and cows. All the butchers visited the farmer, because nowhere else were such well-fed cattle to be found, and it was all due to the work of the little kobold. And as the kobold worked so hard, he hated idleness in others, often playing nasty tricks on the lazy servants, turning the farmhand and maids' clothes inside out and making them a figure of fun, poking and pinching them thoroughly when they failed to get out of bed early. The lazy servants became sullen, complaining loudly about the spirit, left the household and gave it a bad reputation."

Ludwig Bechstein, *Thüringer Sagenbuch*, (Vienna & Leipzig: 1858).

These efforts to ensure diligence were primarily directed at servants and rarely at the head of the household. The house prospered if everyone worked, however, if there was laziness the kobold would eventually leave and take good fortune with him. As a motif in legends passed down through the oral tradition, the protective spirit may have explained domestic affluence, functioning as a mundane explanation for the fortunes, prosperity, and labour of one family or another. This interpretation is closest to that of the kobold as a supernatural ruler of the house. By believing in the existence of kobolds, humans actively surrendered a degree of personal agency. Kobolds provided an explanation for external (harvests) and internal (feuds) influences on daily life, perhaps making some fates easier to bear.

The poltergeist

In some legends, the motif of a protective spirit is missing entirely, replaced by a cheeky pest (*Plagegeist*) which we are familiar with today in the form of *Pumuckl*, from the German children's series created by Ellis Kaut. The kobold plays tricks on humans and animals, annoying them and causing a nuisance to the inhabitants in his house. While the kobold's tricks are often harmless, they can range from simple jokes to the rare life-threatening prank. It can focus its attention on anyone from the children of the household to the servants or even the livestock, but rarely on the head of the household. The activities of the usually invisible kobold are manifest as resounding laughter, the loud opening and closing of doors, and other household noises.

"At night he sent peals of laughter through the stables [of an inn], in the cellar and on the ground, so that the people drew back in fear; he even entered the guest rooms and the dining room. As a result, the inn was frequented less and less, and no one wanted to stay there."

Friedrich Panzer, *Bayerische Sagen und Bräuche*, (Munich: 1855).

Here we see a completely different image of the kobold: a spectre. These legends provide the basis for the terms "*klopfgeist*" or "*poltergeist*"—a knocking ghost or a noisy spirit—a phenomenon which endures into the twenty-first century. At times, a kobold's tedious activities could have far-reaching effects, leading to a disruption in routines and daily tasks, financial hardship, and thus discord between families and loved ones. Some conflicts were even said to have had fatal consequences, while milder manifestations were at least a welcome explanation for accidents in the household:

"There lived a kobold at the Waltersdorf manor, near Berga. It roamed the stables at night, pestered the servants, swapped the horses around in their stalls, but groomed and fed them when the servants were too lazy, broke the maids' milk churns in the cowshed, and played mischievous jokes of all kinds. Once an idle maid sat nonchalantly on a bench; the kobold grabbed her by the hair and pulled so hard she thought she would fall off the bench. Then he exited through the door. When the maid complained to the farmhand about the kobold, she was usually told to give him something, and then he would leave her alone. A farmhand called Salzbrenner worked at the Waltersdorfer farm and liked to get up to no good at night. Once he only returned at midnight, climbing the garden fence to get into the farmyard because the main gate was already locked. The kobold crossed

the entire courtyard to reach him, colliding with Salzbrenner with such force that he fell into the courtyard and was almost unconscious. After nine days he was dead."

Ludwig Bechstein, *Thüringer Sagenbuch*, (Vienna & Leipzig: 1858).

Often the pranks were not meant to be evil in nature but rather instructive and educational. Many protective spirits had teasing characteristics, however, the poltergeist kobold's deliberate destruction of human accomplishments stands in strong contrast to the protective spirit kobold's function. Consequently, narrative researchers assume that this motif may represent a secondary stage in the belief in kobolds. The focus on the power of the kobold to punish employees—in a role akin to the head of the household—may have receded into the background, becoming trivialized as tomfoolery.

"If the cook used the services of a kobold as her secret helper, then each day she had to put down a small bowl of good food in a set place in the house, at a certain time, and then leave it. If she did so, she could relax in the evening, go to bed early, and wake to find her work done in the morning. If, however, she forgot to feed him, she would not only have to do her own work in future, but she also became clumsy—scalding herself with boiling water, breaking pots and dishes, dropping food, so that her master would scold her. The kobold could often be heard laughing and giggling when this happened."

Grimm, Jacob & Wilhelm. *Deutsche Sagen,* (Munich: 1965).

43

The house demon

"It was the year 1518, and the belief amongst our parents in such ghosts was very common, with the Devil having become so tame and secretive that it was not only in the houses that the ghosts could be seen and heard [. . .] and there was almost no house without such a spirit or little Schretel *and little Devil in the form of a young child which caused trouble for people in the kitchen, cellar, stables, cupboards, and everywhere, and also spoke with them."*

Enoch Widmann, *Chronik der Stadt Hof,* (Wurzburg: 2015).

As we have already seen, the Christian Church's battle against superstition also left its mark on the perception of household spirits and shaped the kobold narrative. Under the increasingly strong influence of Christianity, kobolds were declared evil spirits which needed to be exorcised. It is therefore unsurprising that the kobold is described as a companion to witches, and ascribed the characteristics of a *drak*, a flying household spirit connected with fire and falling stars. In his table talk speeches, even Martin Luther reported on the influence of the kobold:

"And as the ghost, as I said, or the wichtlin *(as our people call it) lived in a corner of the kitchen, the kitchen boy was a rogue and poured into the corner dishwater and other filth, hot broth and similar unclean things that were left over and of no use. And the little demon warned the kitchen boy to stop his displeasing activities, but the kitchen boy had no wish to stop. So the kobold and demon became angry and hung the kitchen boy upside down over a beam in the kitchen, but so that his life was not in danger."*

Dr. Martin Luther, *Sämtliche Werke.* Vol. 60-62, (Harvard: 2008) p. 30.

Luther described the demon as a kobold and wichtlin. Although the term *"wichtlin"* is reminiscent of *wichtel*, or dwarf, the description is that of a kobold. Luther regarded ghosts and demons as creatures of the Devil but believed that these spirits were unable to triumph against God and his believers.

But how are the master of the house, the poltergeist, and the house devil as distinct kobold motifs related? Do they represent different perspectives on the same set of beliefs, existing within the first description of kobolds and in parallel since the medieval period?

If we assume that spirits are "projections of human sensitivities and behavioural structures in transcendence," as Erika Lindig describes, then the kobold simply reflects our human nature: ambivalent, neither exclusively good nor evil. It would seem highly likely that the original kobold was an ambivalent creature in popular belief, a ruler of the home, one who brought fortune but could also mete out severe punishment. The Church shifted the focus to the harmful aspects before the kobold found its place in modern popular culture as a mischievous imp and evil, low powered monster in fiction and games.

The Klabautermann

"The Klabautermann is a spirit which all seamen believe in. Before they go aboard a watercraft they carefully listen to see if they can hear knocking. If the klabautermann is onboard, the ship won't go down; if they don't hear knocking then they board the ship unwillingly and with concern."

Karl Bartsch, *Sagen, Märchen und Gebräuche aus Meklenburg 1–2*, (Vienna: 1879) p. 161-162.

The klabautermann is a specific type of kobold, also known as *Kalfatermann*. He usually inhabits sailing ships in the North Sea and Baltic Sea. He is normally invisible, and only the sound of his knocking can be heard, although occasionally he appears as a human of small stature, like his land-bound relatives. He is dressed as a seaman. As a good ship's spirit, he usually does the work of the crew and protects the ship from harm.

"When the ship is at sea, it protects the ship from fire, stranding, and other dangers, and watches over the crew, ensuring they do their duty by boxing the ears of lazy crew members. He requires good food for his services, because he is a connoisseur, preferring the food from the Captain's table."

From Strackerjan, Ludwig (1909): *Aberglaube und Sagen aus dem Herzogtum Oldenburg.* Vol. 1, Oldenburg, p. 486.

The klabautermann first appears after 1800, initially in the literary tales of Heinrich Heine (1797 – 1856), travel books, and a Danish captain's journal, and later in collections of legends from the countries bordering the Baltic Sea and North Sea. During the second half of the nineteenth century, what had begun as a protective spirit amongst seamen had also developed into an ocean spirit which brought misfortune. All in all, the klabautermann is associated with a highly contradictory set of beliefs, although his role as a protective spirit on boats is predominant.

Face-to-face with the Kobold

The kobold's appearance

THE KOBOLD AS A MASTER OF METAMORPHOSIS

There are very few historical depictions of kobolds. However, when described (unless invisible) kobolds appear before humans in a variety of forms. They often take the shape of an animal, with black fur and flaming eyes, or as a small object like a spoon, button, feather, or an orb of light. The anthropomorphic form is, however, the most common. One notable example of a visible and well-documented kobold is the Petermännchen of Schwerin, noted above, for which there is a detailed description which was used to produce etchings and statues.

When creating the models, the primary concern was to amalgamate the various descriptions. To reflect the ambivalent nature of the kobold, four models were produced, each depicting a different motif of the household spirit.

THE COLOUR RED—PLAYING WITH FIRE

Household spirits are often associated with red, the colour of fire. The hearth and stove play a significant role in many demonic legends. In regions such as Saxony, where the character of the kobold merges with that of the fiery house dragon, the kobold is often said to appear in the form of flames.

In some traditions, kobolds are also associated with the so-called *Wichelstein*—a fire guard in the form of a stone wall around primitive stoves. This stone probably gained its ritual association with the stove in the centre of the house at an early stage. The stove effectively represented the heart of the house, the hearth which radiated heat and light.

THE
KOBOLD

SKIN & HAIR

"*The* Petermännchen *was of very small stature, old, wrinkled, but not terrible to look at, with a long, white, pointed beard almost down to the breast, and short, grey, frizzy hair.*"

Karl Bartsch, Sagen, *Märchen und Gebräuche aus Meklenburg 1–2*, (Vienna: 1879) p. 70-71.

Almost without exception, the kobold is depicted as an older figure, with a puckered brow and deeply wrinkled face. The hair is a fiery red or snow white, occasionally grey. The clearly aged kobold may represent experience, knowledge, and wisdom. These were the characteristics included in creating the kobold in our workshop. The sparse, white hair, and colouring typical of an older face, with liver spots was chosen to show wisdom and age.

PHYSIOGNOMY

Kobold proportions are barely human. Short legs, long arms, and above all a large head are typical of the descriptions, plus large, staring eyes to symbolize the kobold's vigilance and scrutinizing gaze. Their inhuman physique was incorporated into the models as well, see that the legs are proportionally much shorter than in humans, the head larger and wider.

PHYSICAL SIZE

Kobolds are rarely large. They usually have a rather small, human-like form. There are almost no details of their actual height: sometimes they are compared to the size of a three or four-year-old child, or they are simply described as "very small" or "tiny."

CLOTHING

A kobold's clothes are described in detail in several legends: in general, they are properly and completely dressed, with a head covering, clothes, and footwear. The clothes themselves vary by region. They may wear coats, frock coats, or a combination of knee-length trousers and a short jacket or waistcoat.

Red clothes, red caps, or red waistcoats are often mentioned. They are also described dressed in grey, as well as green, blue, and black. They wear a diverse range of head coverings, most pointed, and often decorated with feathers or tassels. Footwear may include wooden clogs or slippers, shoes, or boots. Clothes also play a major role in these models, with the significant differences in appearance reflecting their various physical traits.

SEX

"*It should be noted that the house spirits are all male, never female; but there appears to be something genderless in the name.*"

Grimm, Jacob & Wilhelm. *Deutsche Sagen*, (Munich: 1965).

In most legends, kobolds are male creatures. There are only very few legends of female spirits that meet the criteria of a kobold, and they tend to overlap with other spirit beings such as the *Holzfräulein* , or the "little wood woman."

THE PROTECTIVE SPIRIT

The protective spirit is neatly dressed. The clothes may be worn in places but are not scruffy or shabby. Here the combination of knickerbockers and red waistcoat, which is typical of many legends, is used. The waistcoat is made from thick, red wool, under which the kobold wears a light-coloured shirt. The trousers are made from a fine, dark brown wool, leather boots adorn his feet, and he wears a pointed red cap on his head. His eyes look tired, yet he looks steadfastly ahead. The kobold serves, as is his traditional duty.

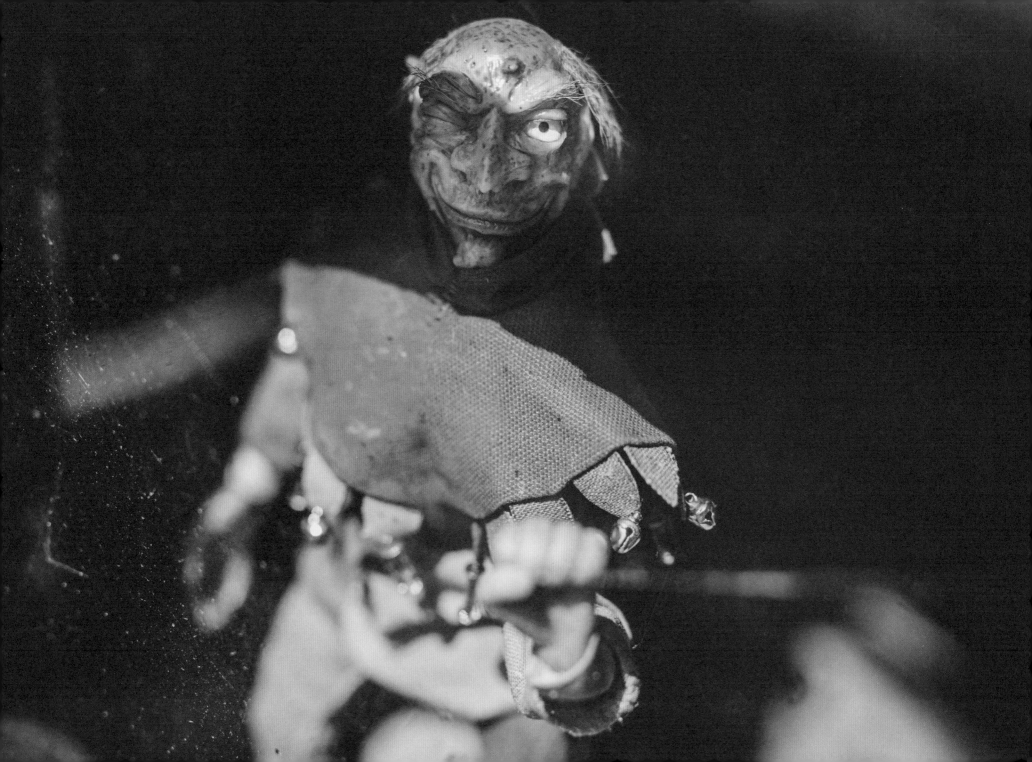

THE POLTERGEIST

Medieval poets such as Konrad von Würzburg and Huge vom Triberg saw the kobold as the embodiment of a fool and performer of mischievous tricks. A document dating to 1250 attests that "kobold" was a nickname given to people of roguish character.

Seen in this light, the kobold has been given features typical of a fool: in designing the clothes the traditional descriptions of kobold dress were deliberately abandoned. Here his garb adopts the style of the medieval mi-parti (vertical separation by colour) in yellow and blue linen. Mi-parti went out of fashion in the late sixteenth century but has remained a characteristic of a fool's clothing to this day. Together with the poulaines, the hint of a tonsure, and the many bells, the outfit as a whole picks up on many of the motifs of a fool. The hourglass symbolizes the transient nature of human life and is typical of medieval illustrations. The fool is also seen as a symbol of this transience.

Finally, the stance of the poltergeist indicates his primary function: playing jokes, knocking, and punishing. The left hand raised, ready to knock, the kobold winks at the viewer with a mischievous grin on his face.

THE HOUSE DEMON

The house demon's clothes are those of a "protective spirit" but are significantly more worn and dirtier. Tormented by the Church and branded a devilish demon, the household spirit's original association with fire remains, with burn holes and scorched material referencing the spirit's devilish origins.

The head displays the typical "Devil's horns," the eyes are those of a snake, with pointed pupils. His smile is malicious, the index finger raised, enticing the viewer, while the other hand holds a rose: a symbol of transience and yet perhaps with the prospect of a pact to be concluded.

THE KLABAUTERMANN

Although often invisible, when the klabautermann reveals himself, he is usually dressed in the clothes of a seaman and sailor. The style mirrors historic marine uniforms, with a double row of buttons and matching cap.

Patches of salt on the fabric and boots are evidence of adventures had at sea, as the klabautermann accompanies crews on their journeys across the oceans, usually protecting them and warning of danger.

Nonchalantly enjoying his pipe, the ship spirit's weather-beaten face is looking out to sea.

STAYING ALIVE: THE KOBOLD IN POP CULTURE

"Apart from a few remains, the legends of the kobold, the Pöpel, going about his activities in the house, stable, and barn, have largely disappeared from the memories of today's population. The new buildings which are gradually replacing the old and dilapidated ruins have caused him to be forgotten."
Karl Spiegel, *Die bayerischen Sagen vom Kobold,* (München: 1916).

Our houses have changed, and with them their spirit, culture, and beliefs. Many of the creatures of popular mythology appear to have been forgotten today. However, the kobold has fared better than many other creatures in this respect, although his protective and morally instructive nature has almost entirely disappeared from the modern kobold narrative. He is now seen as a dwarf-like spirit fond of jokes and pranks, as the Duden definition shows:

"In popular belief a dwarf-like spirit found in the house and farm, with a penchant for amusing pranks, yet occasionally evil and deceitful."
Karl Spiegel, *Die bayerischen Sagen vom Kobold,* (München: 1916).

In 1962, the German audio series, *Master Eder and his Pumuckl*, brought the kobold back into the world of children. The series was based on the books of the same name by Ellis Kaut, and for years was followed by books, records, films, TV series, and musicals. *Pumuckl* completely corresponds to the modern, child-friendly image of a household spirit. His mischievous nature determines his actions, while his origins in ancestral cults and veneration as a protective power are entirely absent. With a nod to his activities as a helper in the household, in 1929 the Vorwerk company developed its first electric hand-held vacuum cleaner and named it kobold because it's handy within the household.

Today, direct references to the old legends remain in just a few places: in Schwerin the Petermännchen is harnessed for marketing purposes and has become part of the town's identity. People regularly dress as the Petermännchen at events or on city tours, while from 2006 to 2011 a Petermännchen museum honoured this legendary figure and shared this tidbit of culture with residents and visitors alike.

Since 2001, the municipality of Pinnow, near Schwerin, has incorporated the Petermännchen into its municipal coat of arms.

The Pinnow (Mecklenburg) coat of arms. From Schütt, Hans-Heinz (2002): Auf Schild und Siegel, CW publishing group, Schwerin.

Piotr Siedlecki, *Wicked Elf,* digital, 2012.

When we think of the kobold today, our mind is immediately drawn to the traditional Irish kobold, with the appearance of the leprechaun. In pop culture the leprechaun is an ambivalent creature: it may promise treasure at the end of a rainbow, yet since 1993 it has also been the antagonist in the series of horror films of the same name.

The kobold, like many other mythological figures, has found its way into modern fantasy culture, although in a completely modified form: the first pen-and-paper role-playing game, *Dungeons & Dragons*, published in 1974, entirely altered the traditional image of the kobold. The game described the kobold as a lizard-like, evil monster, which appears in groups and lays traps for humans. The game's inventors could hardly have moved further away from the kobold's folklore origins.

Mariana Ruiz Villarreal, *Kobold Rat Master*, 2012, RPGWiki.

AT HOME BY THE STOVE AND OVEN—THE SITE OF KOBOLD ACTIVITY

Kobolds are directly connected to their families. As the spirit with the closest personal relationships with humans, they appear in a variety of locations associated with human activity, from splendid palaces to the most run-down barn. They serve the nobility, as well as peasants and commoners. Churches and monasteries were also subjected to the mischievous activities of kobolds; they were also seen in stables and workshops. Mills have always been particularly magical places, encouraging people in many regions to tell tales of the spirits inhabiting these buildings.

"The house spirits were found at the stove and oven at night. When the fire burned bright, they could not be seen; when only the glowing embers remained could the house spirits be seen in the half-light."

Karl Spiegel, *Die bayerischen Sagen vom Kobold*, (München: 1916).

In the house itself, kobolds were mainly found in the kitchen. The stove was regarded as the home of the kobold, the red of its clothing associated with the fire. The stove and hearth play a major role in many demonological legends. In regions such as Saxony, where the figure of the kobold merged with that of the fiery drak, the kobold is often said to have a blazing appearance.

In some traditions, kobolds are also associated with the so-called *Wichelstein*—a fire guard in the form of a stone wall around primitive stoves. This stone probably gained its ritual association with the stove in the centre of the house at an early stage. The stove effectively represented the heart of the house, the hearth which radiated heat and light.

"A farmer's wife placed bread and milk in the Wichelstein for the household spirits. When her son abandoned this tradition, loud complaints were heard emanating from the stove at night: the household spirits left the town, and the house lost its fortune and blessings."

Karl Spiegel, *Die bayerischen Sagen vom Kobold*, (München: 1916).

The Wichtel

"When you want the [wichtel] to work for you, you go to the *Strazel* hole and call: 'Hey, come here, you'll get something to eat, but you'll need to work!' Then they come in the night. You put soup and bread on the table, and the little creatures eat everything, however much you provide. They are especially fond of bread and milk [. . .] They work extremely hard, but no one is permitted to watch them. In the house where the narrator of this tale served, they threshed the wheat: they had often laid the grains on the threshing floor by the time the people arrived. In the house they did the dishes [. . .] They have an exceptionally good sense of hearing, are quick, and extremely shy. People watched through cracks in the door as they ate. They always appeared in groups."

Franz Schönwerth. *Aus der Oberpfalz. Sitten und Sagen.* Vol. 2, (Augsburg: 1858), p. 298–299.

Hardworking Helpers from the Mountains

In contrast to kobolds, wichtel—often translated as gnome, or imp—are both male and female, they usually appear in groups of at least two or three, and they are not bound to a single family or farm. Instead, they live in their own communities below the earth in mountain and rock caves, far from humans, earning them the name *Unterirdische*, or "underground people."

From here they come into human houses where they serve as friendly, benevolent household spirits—unless mistreated. They bring fortune and prosperity to the home, farm, and workshop.

NAMES: REGIONAL VARIATIONS

Over time, dozens of different names arose for the creatures who live under the mountains. In Central Germany, the term "wichtel" or "wichtelmännchen" was predominant. These small creatures are also known outside the region as Zwerge, or dwarfs. People are also familiar with the term "heinzelmännchen," from August Kopisch's *Die Heinzelmännchen von Köln*, known further afield as "The Elves of Cologne." Sometimes legends refer to a kobold as a heinzelmännchen, or hinzemännchen, although these beings do not meet the functional criteria of a wichtel.

In addition to these popular designations, there is also a whole series of regional names associated with the wichtel. This is largely a reflection of local dialects, but also includes significant variations.

The "small, hardworking man" as a caricature within folklore has a long history. But here we must be careful, because according to modern narrative researchers, the nineteenth century image of the wichtel and heinzelmännchen are based on different ideas and traditions, not always related, but both feeding into the wichtel narrative.

The Old High German name, wicht, which date to the tenth century, demonstrate the origins of the German wicht or wichtel, and the English wight. The original meaning of "wicht" was "thing." In a certain sense, the wicht was a "reified" demon whose real name was taboo and thus never spoken because people feared that calling a demon by its name would summon it.

Yet our modern image of dwarfs as old, bearded, combative beings is relatively recent, established during the German Romantic period as dwarfs found their way into contemporary art and fiction. Illustrations of wichtel in the collections of folktales by the Brothers Grimm established the image of the dwarf worldwide, providing the basis for later interpretations by Walt Disney (1901 – 1966) and J.R.R. Tolkien (1892 – 1973). Their modified images of dwarfs have left a permanent stamp on modern fantasy literature.

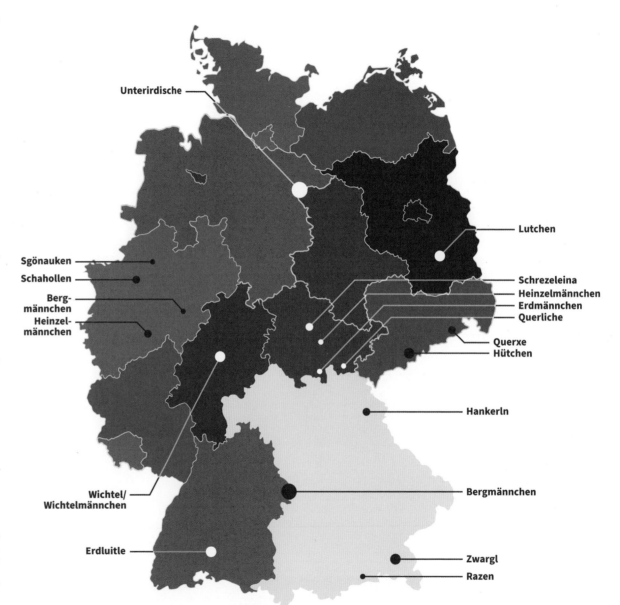

NAME VARIANTS OF THE WICHTEL WITHIN GERMANY

Unterirdische

Lutchen

Sgönauken

Schahollen

Berg-männchen

Heinzel-männchen

Schrezeleina

Heinzelmännchen

Erdmännchen

Querliche

Querxe

Hütchen

Hankerln

Wichtel/ Wichtelmännchen

Bergmännchen

Erdluitle

Zwargl

Razen

A cultural scientific analysis of the dwarf motif could fill an entire book on its own. Dwarf-like figures appear in Greek mythology and the Old Norse *Prose Edda*, as well as the Middle High German heroic epics and courtly poetry of the medieval period. In the *Nibelungenlied* "The Song of the Nibelungs," which first appeared around the year 1200), the dwarf Alberich guards the Nibelung treasure, losing it to the hero Siegfried. Alberich (also known as Auberon in the Old French legend of Huon de Bordeaux) later becomes Shakespeare's Oberon in *A Midsummer Night's Dream* (1595), who gains fame as the king of the fairies in Arthurian legend.

Oberon and the dwarfs of courtly literature were nearly godlike and magical, often represented in their own wild realms of forest or grand underground realms. Their impact was on those lofty humans, the princes and princesses of the court. Conversely, the wichtel and heinzelmännchen in nineteenth century legends remain described as mountain or household spirits living within or close to the human realm impacting the daily lives of the average citizen.

Alberich seduces the Lombard queen, woodcut, in *Heldenbuch* (Strassburg: Johann Prüss, 1480).

While people including Konrad von Megenberg (1309 – 1374) tried as early as the fourteenth century to provide a scientific explanation for the existence of dwarfs and other demons, the physician and natural philosopher Paracelsus regarded the earth spirits as godly creatures, giving them the name "gnome." He derived the name—although incorrectly—from the Greek *gēnomos*, or earth-dweller. His writing was so influential that the term gnome is now widespread in both science and popular belief.

More recently, it was the legends of the heinzelmännchen of Köln which served to keep the motif of the wichtel alive. The first written evidence of these spirit servants appears in 1826, with Ernst Weyden (1805 – 1869), an author from Köln, recording the legends dating from Köln's early history, in his work *Cölns Vorzeit*. Weyden set the events in his tales in the late eighteenth century.

LadyofHats, *D&D Dwarf*, 2016, WikiMedia Commons.

"It is not over fifty years since the heinzelmännchen, as they are called, used to live and perform their exploits in Köln. They were little naked men who used to do all sorts of work: bake bread, wash, and suchlike housework. So it is said, but no one ever saw them. In the time that the heinzelmännchen were still there, there was in Köln many a baker who kept no man, for the little people used always to make, overnight, as much black and white bread as the baker wanted for his shop. In many houses they used to wash and do all their work for the maids. Now, about this time, there was an expert tailor to whom they appeared to have taken a great fancy, for when he married, he found in his house, on the wedding-day, the finest victuals and the most beautiful vessels and utensils, which the little folk had stolen elsewhere and brought to them. When, with time, the tailor's family increased, the little ones used to give the tailor's wife considerable aid in her household affairs, they washed for her, and on holidays and festival times they scoured the copper and tin, and the house from the garret to the cellar. If at any time the tailor had a press of work, he was sure to find it already done for him in the morning by the heinzelmännchen. Curiosity began now to torment the tailor's wife, and she was dying to get a look at the heinzelmännchen, but do what she would, she could never accomplish it. One time, she threw peas all down the stairs that they might fall and hurt themselves, and that so she might see them next morning. But this project missed, and since that time the heinzelmännchen have totally disappeared, as has the case been everywhere, owing to the curiosity of people, which always has been the destruction of so much of what was beautiful in the world. The heinzelmännchen, in consequence of this, went off all in a body out of the town, with music playing, but people could only hear the music, for no one could see the small men, who forthwith got into a ship and went away, whither no one knows. The good times, however, are said to have disappeared from Köln along with the heinzelmännchen."

Thomas Keightley, *The Fairy Mythology.* Vol. II, (London: 1833).

Theodor Mintrop, *The King of the Heinzelmänner with Anna in the kitchen*, wood engraving, in *Die Gartenlaube* (Leipzig: Ernst Keil, 1875) p.145.

The heinzelmännchen are unable to cope with human curiosity and leave the area. Weyden's texts created the basis upon which the oral tradition of the heinzelmännchen legends would thrive. However, these little helpers only achieved immortality after 1836 and August Kopisch's (1799 – 1853) poem, *Die Heinzelmännchen von Köln*: "Once upon a time in Köln, how comfortable it was with the Heinzelmen!" Since then, the heinzelmännchen have provided the ideal figure for advertising everything from products to cities. The poem was often reprinted and has been translated into many languages.

The population of Köln identified so strongly with its household spirits that the city's improvement association paid for a fountain, the *heinzelmännchenbrunnen*, to mark Kopisches' 100th birthday. Built near the cathedral and sited opposite Köln's oldest brewer, the fountain features eight reliefs portraying the work of the nocturnal helpers, above whom stands the tailor's wife.

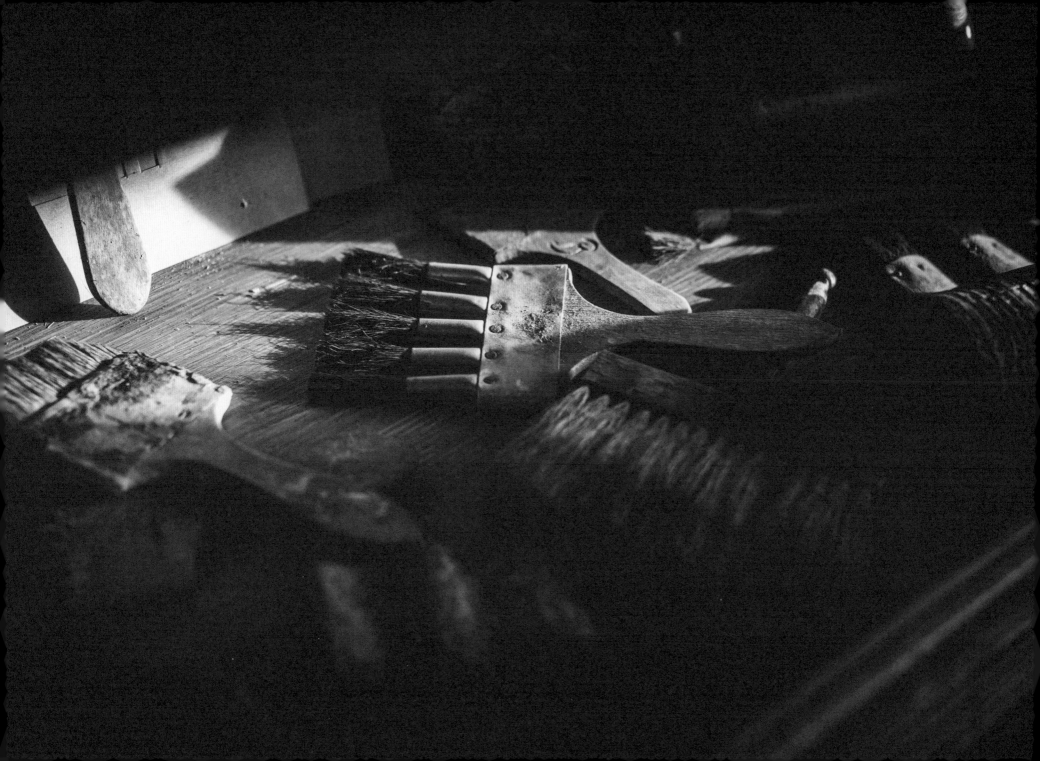

Through their actions, wichtel bring fortune and prosperity to our workshops. If they leave the house, the loss of wealth and wellbeing will usually follow.

Little Grey Men in the Stove

The wichtel's appearance

OFTEN DESCRIBED, RARELY ILLUSTRATED

There are almost no images of wichtel and dwarfs in their function as household spirits dating from the medieval period. Even the very few illustrations available often blend with those of other demons and devilish beings. The most nuanced descriptions of the wichtel are found in nineteenth and twentieth-century collections of legends. Many artistic representations were also created during this period, such as the reliefs on Köln's heinzelmännchen fountain. In 1995, folklorist Dagmar Linhart collated many of these legends, analyzing them for Franconian household spirits, which included the wichtel.

Linhart's research revealed many important findings that extended beyond Bavaria. One key historical source was the collection by Franz Schönwerth, who examined the customs and legends of the Oberpfalz, including highly detailed descriptions of the appearance of wichtel, heinzelmännchen, and dwarfs in his books. Schönwerth's detailed descriptions, together with a series of other traditions, give us an idea of how wichtel may have been perceived. The following interpretations combine various attributes and attempt to unify the often-contradictory details to create a consistent image.

THE
WICHTEL

SKIN & HAIR

"According to the landlady, these Schrazen were about two feet tall, with snow white hair and red eyes, which explains why they couldn't bear daylight."

Franz Schönwerth. *Aus der Oberpfalz. Sitten und Sagen.* Vol. 2, (Augsburg: 1858) p. 297.

Wichtel are often described as little grey, black, or red men and women, although it is not clear if this refers to the colour of their skin or their clothing. Some legends describe snow white skin, others dark skin tones akin to the "Moors." As lighter skin was the more common descriptor, and often associated with red eyes, these are the characteristic features used here.

PHYSICAL SIZE

"They are built like children, very small, around one-and-a-half feet tall, so that fourteen of them can work in an oven at once, and they are dressed like farmers."

Franz Schönwerth. *Aus der Oberpfalz. Sitten und Sagen.* Vol. 2, (Augsburg: 1858) p. 298.

Thus, representations of wichtel are usually small. The legends tell of anything from a "half step" to the size of a newborn. In many places comparisons with an oven are frequently cited as a means of describing their size: In Heiden (Westphalia) seven wichtel fit into an oven to work, in the Oberpfalz up to fourteen. After measuring historic ovens and realizing their sizes vary, it was decided to present wichtels as fourteen cm tall—so that anywhere between seven and ten wichtel could truly fit into a historic oven.

CLOTHING

"[The Zwargl] look like little people, the men with long beards, the women very old, dressed in thick grey over-alls, with short arms and legs, and wide heads. Although hardly as tall as a pair of shoes, they are very strong. They can make themselves visible or invisible. They used to be seen often."

Franz Schönwerth. *Aus der Oberpfalz. Sitten und Sagen.* Vol. 2, (Augsburg: 1858) p. 325.

The cut of the wichtel's dress often mirrored that of the local rural population. They often wore coat-like skirts, some made from rush mats, some from coarse fabric. A broad, pointed hat—often part of the coat itself but sometimes a separate hat or cap—was also part of their uniform. Wichtel usually wore coarse linen, threadbare fabrics, worn wooden slippers, and generally appear in a pitiable state. Their colours are red, black, and especially grey, colours similar to those associated with kobolds.

The wichtel's clothes are based on patterns for historic coats, creating a piece of clothing which could be described as a "coat-like skirt." Here, coarse woollen material lined with ecru-coloured linen was used. A pointed hood and long, rolled-up sleeves complete the outfit.

SEX

In contrast to kobolds, there exist both male and female wichtel. Therefore, both sexes are represented in the figures we created (p. 81).

THE SWEEPER AND THE CARPET BEATER

However heavy or tedious the work may be, the wichtel complete their duties conscientiously and at high speed. The *Hennessenmännchen* once lived on the Hennessenberg near Bonn. If a farmer had not finished his work, then he went to the hill in the evening and told the little men what still needed to be cleaned, washed, or finished. By morning, the invisible helpers had usually completed everything.

THE SEAMSTRESS

"In the evenings, in a house in the Johannesgasse, a male wichtel would often sit with the women who were spinning and help them, often spooling their reels through the night. No one saw the little men. Then along came Andres Babst, who was born on a Sunday at the pealing of the bells during the Lord's Prayer and therefore saw more than other people. He saw the little elf and asked, 'Hey, who's that little old [...] man over there, behind the tiled stove, helping the young girl spin?' The little man made an angry grimace, disappeared, and never helped again."

Christian Ludwig Wucke, *Sagen der mittleren Werra.* Vol. 2, (Norderstedt: 1864).

THE GRAIN BEARER

It is notable how many legends tell of wichtel as bearers of grain. Usually, the little helpers transport a single ear of wheat, or a small bundle, which they laboriously carry to a granary normally belonging to a poor farmer. But appearances are deceptive: once in the granary, the ears of wheat multiply. Ungrateful people who mock the spirit as he struggles with his load reap anger in return, becoming the subject of the wichtel's bitter revenge.

"In olden days, there lived a miller at the mill in Lindes an der Saale whom the wichtel had made a rich man, his granary always full of grain. Once a wichtel climbed the stairs to the warehouse floor. Although only carrying a single ear of wheat, he squealed plaintively and continually. The miller became angry and called: 'You lazy moaner, how you complain about your ear of wheat!' In response to this coarse speech, the wichtel carried all the grain away, making the miller a poor man."

Alexander Schöppner, *Sagenbuch der bayerischen Lande*, (Munich: 1866).

THE BAKER

Some wichtel are reported to have stolen food, others were happy to receive a little food as a tribute. Wichtel were particularly difficult to deal with, but very easy to drive away, as the following tale from Thüringen shows:

"Helpful dwarfs brought great prosperity to the Rauda mill near Eisenberg, for as long as they were given clean bowls of fruit, bread, or cake. Once they were heard moaning and panting all night in the mill, making the sound of mice squeaking. The miller's wife had added caraway seeds to the bread, making the wichtel ill. In response, they left the mill, and the prosperous days were over."

Robert Eisel, *Sagenbuch des Voigtlandes,* (Gera: 1871).

THE DWARFS LEAVE—NO CHANCE OF RETURN?

"South of Spichra [Thüringen], on the righthand bank of the Werra begins the Spatenberg, in which is a hole in the ground called the Wichtelkutte. *Here many wichtel have lived for a long time. But one beautiful morning two little men came to the ferryman Beck in Spichra, demanding that he take them across, and went with him to the river. When they were on the ferry and the ferryman was just about to push off from the bank, they asked him to wait a couple of minutes; but no one came. Yet the ferry sank deeper and deeper into the water, became heavier and heavier, and when the ferryman finally set off, he realized he had never carried a heavier load. Once he reached the righthand bank, the ferry became lighter again.*

"'Now, tell me, ferryman, how much will you charge for our passage?' asked one of the little men. 'Do you want to be paid with coin per head, or with a bushel of salt?' As one bushel of salt seemed a much richer payment than the fee for transporting two people, this is what the ferryman chose. 'You would have done better to have charged per person! Look over my right shoulder,' said the little man, and when the ferryman did so he saw countless numbers of little people who had climbed from the ferry and milled around on the bank. But as the first two little men climbed off the ferry, they all became invisible to the ferryman. However, when he turned, he found a full bushel of pure salt on the ferry, and over time the bushel never became empty. The wichtel set off, but no one knew where they went."

Ernst Karl Wenig, *Thüringer Sagen,* (Rudolstadt: 1992).

Just as on the riverbanks of the Werra, the dwarfs and heinzelmännchen in many other parts of Europe left their homes and moved on. This motif of the dwarf migration (in German: *Zwergenauszug*), as well as dwarf ferry passengers, is widespread, and characteristic for the wichtel type of household spirit. The reasons, however, differ widely: sometimes it was grounded in the actions of the people, such as bakers adding caraway seeds to the bread, or treating the helpful spirits with disrespect; sometimes however it was the introduction of Christianity, the first sounding of church bells, and the spread of the Enlightenment which caused the wichtel to leave for new pastures. In terms of cultural history, it was generally accepted that it was

the Enlightenment and enlightened absolutism which rang the death knell for the belief in spirits and demons. The wichtel probably disappeared with the transition to an enlightened society during the Industrial Age. Many narrative researchers now assume that such "end motifs" were an attempt to retain the legends' plausibility, by assigning the events to a time in the distant past. The disappearance of the wichtel was a (more or less) believable reason for their absence in the present day.

"As everything became livelier, as the forests were cut down, and as people increasingly failed to ask about them, they moved away to the east, into the mountains."
Paul Zaunert, *Westfälische Sagen,* (Jena: 1927).

Yet that might not be the entire reason. Let us take a last critical look at the genesis of the wichtel legends in the following text:

"The passage of time and spreading Enlightenment finally drove these creatures away. The local inhabitants looked sad and wistful as the wichtel said their good-byes and took off, spending all night being transported across the Elster by a fisherman near Köstritz. Since their departure, the locals say, the goods times are over for the region."
Robert Eisel, *Sagenbuch des Voigtlandes*, (Gera: 1871).

Quotes like this tell us perhaps less about the actual beliefs of the society, and more about those who recorded these tales: in the collections of legends compiled in the nineteenth century, authors and collectors had a nostalgic vision of their own cultural past. It was a time of romance, a fictitious concept of a better, happier age.

Were the legends of wichtel and dwarfs a criticism of globalization, industrialization, and political developments? This is suggested by the renowned artist Carl Spitzweg in his 1848 painting *Gnome Watching Railway Train*, which contrasted the unspoiled natural environment with technical advances in the changing world. There is nothing new about our human tendency to glorify the past, defining ourselves by countries, borders, and supposed histories in which everything was once better.

The nostalgic longing for a wonderful past is not a new phenomenon and has always been exploited by politicians and marketing departments. Studies show just how

Carl Spitzweg, *Gnome Watching Railway Train*, oil on wood, 1848.

strongly our daily decision-making can be swayed by the glorified past, whether to influence who we vote for or what we buy. It was no different when the Brothers Grimm, Bechstein, and Schönwerth were alive. Politics and marketing worked through stories. That makes the wichtel legends a fascinating testimony to past social policy.

THE LITTLE GREY MAN
BY DANIEL ROTHGEB

There was once a baker
In Pirmasens, as you know,
And at night during the witching hour
He was assisted by a little grey man.

He heated the oven, worked hard,
Covered the floor, sieved the flour,
And did everything so quickly
Producing perfect bread and rolls.

The baker often overslept,
Waking in a foul mood,
But when he saw his work was done,
He was delighted and his heart was full!

He grinned and thought
How lucky he was to have an apprentice
Requiring neither food nor pay,
And worth more than a dozen others.

But the baker wanted to see
His clever and quick helper at work,
So, he decided to stay up late and watch,
But what was the best way to do so?

Then he had an idea,
He would please the little chap
By presenting him with a little red skirt
As quickly as possible, ideally today.

The little grey man arrived,
Ready to start his work,
Then the baker stepped out
And stood before him.

He held out the little skirt,
Ready to express his thanks
For the services performed,
But suddenly—the little man was gone!

He waited but the little man was gone
And he realized that,
From now on,
He would have to do the work himself.

When he heated the oven each night,
And made his own dough,
Standing there, tired and sweating,
Was he thinking about the little man?

Alexander Schöppner, *Sagenbuch der bayerischen Lande*, (Munich: 1866) p. 353-354f.

The dreadful state of a wichtel's clothing often led well-intentioned people to present them with clothes. However, the gift itself would cause the wichtel to put down their tools and, now "paid off," leave the house, never to return. The gift would cause the wichtel to cease their work either because they had been discovered and confronted, or because they had been compensated for their work, signaling that their presence was no longer wanted or required.

"Once a couple of wichtel men resided in a mill in Brotterrode (Thüringen) where they helped the mill's owners, a pair of brothers, by sharpening and polishing many blades every evening, so that by the next morning they were exhausted [. . .] The brothers wanted to express their gratitude and—having once listened and noticed that the wichtel were very badly dressed—had little red jackets and blue trousers made for the wichtel. These they left by the blades one evening [. . .] Soon the wichtel arrived to start their work. But when they saw the clothes, they were saddened, and said: "There is our payment, now we have to leave!" They took the gift, left, and were never seen again."

Christian Ludwig Wucke, *Sagen der mittleren Werra.* Vol. 2, (Norderstedt: 1864).

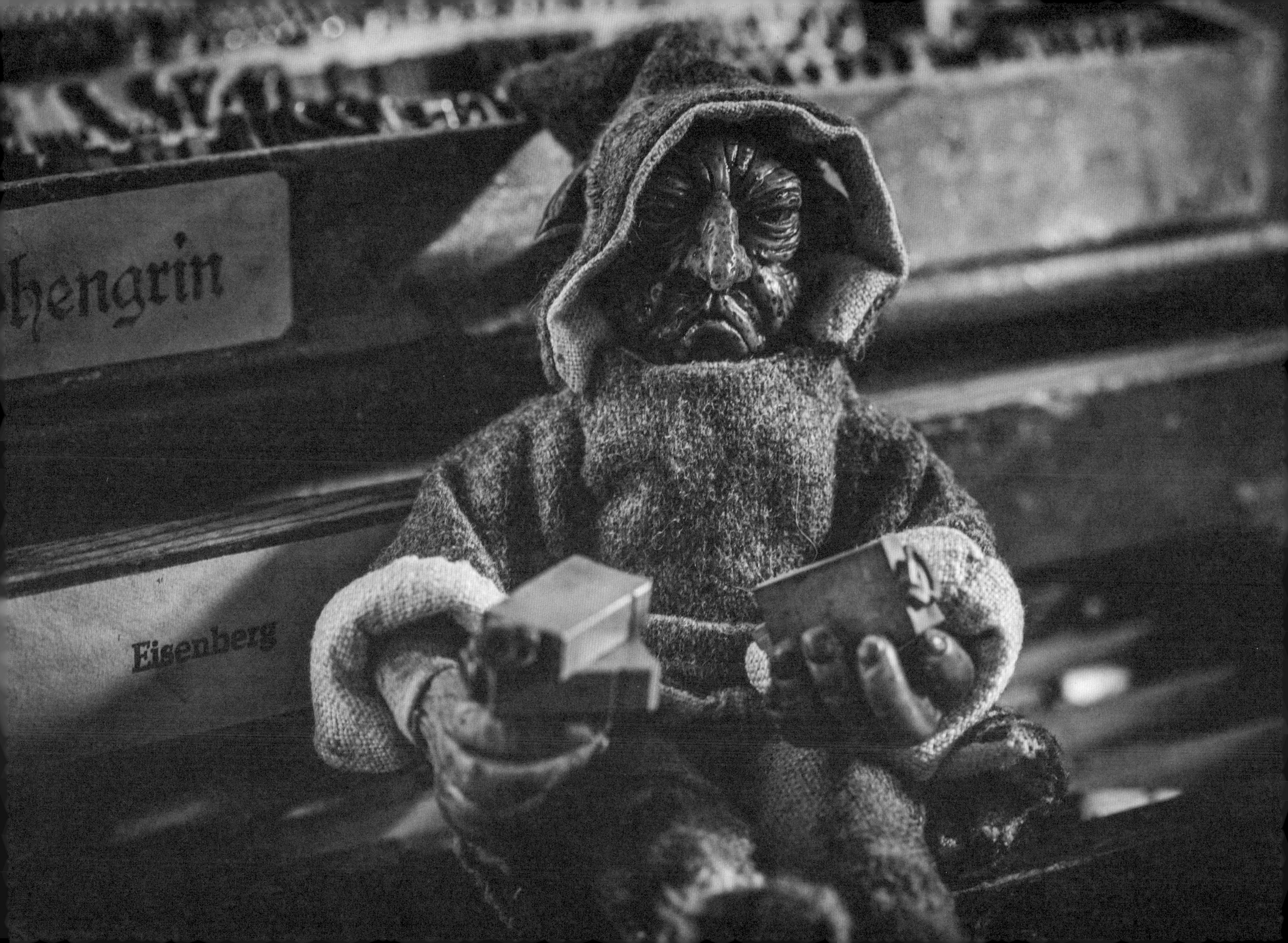
hengrin
Eisenberg

The Drak

"The dragons appear as fiery figures and are classified into good and evil dragons. Most fall down the chimney into the house in the form of a fireball, releasing their treasures, milk, eggs, and money on the ground. Those were known as the good dragons [. . .] When good dragons were allowed into the house, the milk churns were quickly cleaned, and then placed in the kitchen and cellar where the dragon could pour in its milk. To attract a dragon, the butter churns were made from types of wood believed holy during pagan times: juniper, mallow, lime."

Ludwig Bechstein, *Deutsches Sagenbuch*, (Leipzig: 1853), p. 374.

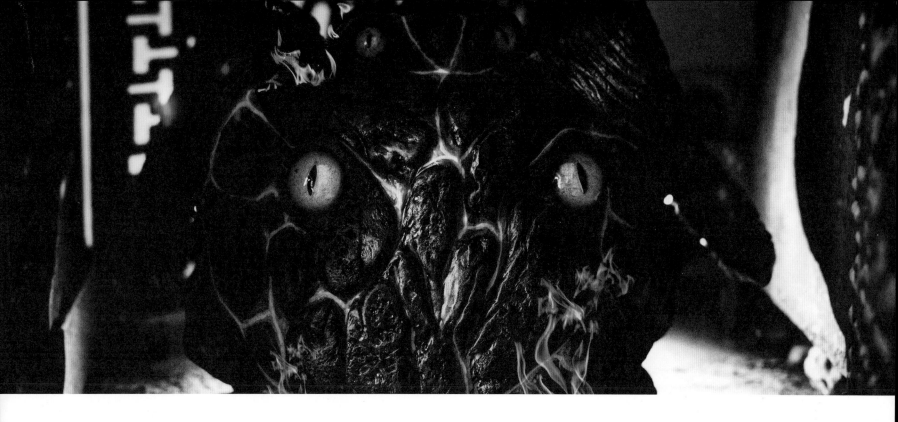

Fiery Assistants Bring Rapid Prosperity

The drak is a flying household spirit, primarily found in Northern and Central Germany. It made farmers prosperous by bringing grains, milk, and gold down the chimney. In Western culture there is a saying: "Do you think money grows on trees?" In Germany, the lore of the drak in one such old adage, in German: "*Du denkst wohl, uns fliegt's Geld zur Feueresse rein?*" or, "You think the fire-eater flies in, bringing money?"

Dragons of German folklore include a multitude of demon-like beasts that vary widely in appearance and activity, and they often have unrecognizable shared origins. They are grouped into two main classes of dragons: winged serpents and household spirits. The small, helpful household spirit dragon should not be confused with the large and mythical beasts we know from heroic battles of myth, legends, and fantasy. Their similar names and joint presence in legends have led to convergence in their appearance and alignment in their characteristics: we occasionally find the drak on two legs and with a human face, as a protector of treasure. Although they may share some characteristics, the wealth of different features is much greater, which makes it unlikely that the drak and the dragons of Arthurian legend and contemporary fantasy share origins.

A DRAGON IN THE HOUSE

"One only finds this mixture of wings and Alraun (dragon) in Northern Germany, where popular etymology has transformed the original drak into a dragon!"

Hanns Bächtold-Stäubli et al., *Handwörterbuch des deutschen Aberglaubens*, (Berlin/Leipzig: 1927) p. 395f.

Just like the other household spirits, there are several variations on the name drak, each reflecting their local origins. However, many of these are typical kobold names. Interestingly, in Saxony the two beings, kobold and house dragon, merge at an early stage due to their functional similarities. In West Saxony, for example, the terms "kobold" and "dragon" were fully synonymous amongst the peasants. However, this was extremely unusual in other regions, as the creatures were dissimilar in both appearance and associated characteristics. It is thought that the term "drak" or "*Drakel*" might have its etymological origins in the Latin *Mandragora* or mandrake.

OF WITCH TRIALS AND FOLKTALES

The primary sources for the activity of the fiery house dragons for the period between 1500 and 1800 were the witch trials, and the reports of fires allegedly started by the fiery dragon. They reflect a strong belief in these household spirits, as immortalized in nineteenth-century collections of legends. One of the oldest records comes from Johannes Agricola (~1494 – 1566) dating from 1529, in which he notes in his collection of sayings:

"The Devil is also a dragon / who steals from other people / and who brings them things / one has to give them food and drink."

Johannes Agricola, *Das ander teyl gemainer Tewtscher Sprichwörter, mit ihrer außlegung hat fünffthalb hundert newer Wörtter*, (Nuremberg: 1529).

For Agricola, a friend and pupil of Martin Luther who was significantly influenced by the Reformation, the house dragon—like all other demonic beings—was an embodiment of the Devil himself. Further important sources are provided in later folktales which report on the characteristics of the drak and its influence on people. In many legends the dragons fly at night. This description probably arises as

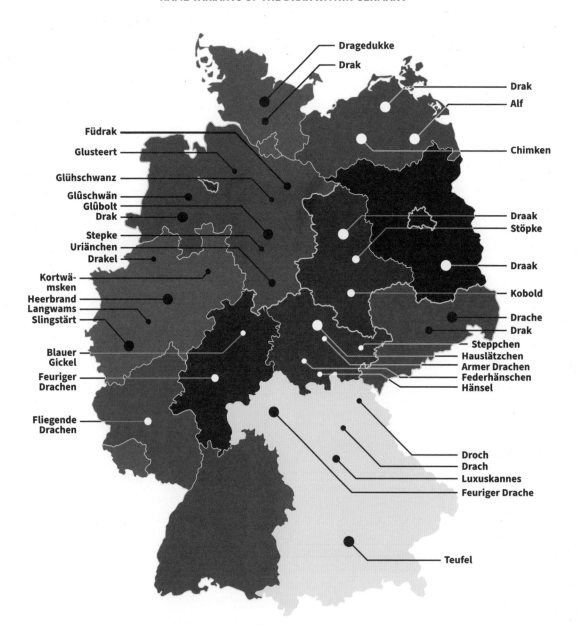

NAME VARIANTS OF THE DRAK WITHIN GERMANY

Dragedukke
Drak
Drak
Alf
Füdrak
Glusteert
Chimken
Glühschwanz
Glûschwän
Glûbolt
Drak
Draak
Stöpke
Stepke
Uriänchen
Drakel
Draak
Kortwä-msken
Kobold
Heerbrand
Langwams
Drache
Slingstärt
Drak
Steppchen
Hauslätzchen
Blauer Gickel
Armer Drachen
Federhänschen
Feuriger Drachen
Hänsel
Fliegende Drachen
Droch
Drach
Luxuskannes
Feuriger Drache
Teufel

a means of explaining shooting stars, lightning, and other fiery manifestations of the sky and heavens. When shooting stars crossed the sky it was said the drak was bringing money to evil people. Flames jumping from a chimney or sparks flying from the fire were also interpreted as indications of its arrival. It was assumed that wherever the drak went, he would scorch his path, and, when insufficiently cared for, his own place of residence. The appearance of a drak was said to be a sign of a future conflagration. The dictionary of German superstition says:

"[. . .] the winged dragon spews fire; the house spirit is fire."

Hanns Bächtold-Stäubli et al., *Handwörterbuch des deutschen Aberglaubens,* (Berlin/Leipzig: 1927) p. 39.

A drak was a threat for those who failed to suitably recompense it for its services because it meant the drak might set fire to the house and cause devastation.

"When you see the dragon entering the house via the chimney and then wear a slipper on the wrong foot or put the wheel the wrong way round on the wagon, then the dragon cannot get out again, and burns down the house. Once he has finished burning, he sits on the fence and laughs to himself."

Leander Petzoldt, *Deutsche Volkssagen*, (Wiesbaden: 2007) p. 254.

Many documents, most dating from the seventeenth century, claim that the drak was responsible for fires in houses as well as whole districts in towns such as Leipzig, Coburg, Liegnitz, and Schleiz. Christianization served to underscore a close association between the drak and the Devil, with figures like Luther making the connection in their writings. Those who believed in the drak were accused of witchcraft and Devil worship.

One woman from Coburg was asked during questioning: "Does your amour often appeared to you in the form of a dragon?" In 1714, the Kirstens, a married couple in Dresden, were accused of being owners of such a drak. What sort of person would own a house dragon? In the eyes of the Catholic Church, it would only be evil people who had entered a pact with the Devil, as well as witches, sorcerers, or Jesuits. Consequently, breaking free from the Devil was only possible through a blessing, holy water, prayer, confession, or another form of aid provided by members of the Church.

MONEY, GRAIN, MILK—
WHAT WAS THE BENEFIT OF A DRAGON IN THE HOUSE?

The house dragon had different functions. It brought money and grain, as well as butter or milk and it protected its master's property.

In Germany and the Slavic countries, the drak is primarily seen as a money demon whose purpose was to bring gold and treasure. This is particularly clear through its association with the geldmännlein, the little money man, and the way in which the dragon might be acquired. There are some variations in legend, but if someone found a coin and stored it safely, then it was reputed to double in value from day to day, finally turning into a special taler, a German silver coin. If the taler was then picked up, a dragon would arrive. If one found a dragon at a crossroads at midnight, and fed it with gruel, then it would produce a piece of gold every hour.

If the house dragon brought corn instead of money, then it was a grain, wheat or corn demon which functioned as a household spirit. It would help in threshing the wheat, as a legend from Rügen tells:

"A farmer's wife at mass failed to swallow the host, instead taking it secretly out of her mouth and mixing it with the feed for her cows at home. This obliged the dragon to bring her riches. The villagers of Trebnitz and Schwaara also became rich."

Dietrich Kühn, *Sagen und Legenden aus Thüringen,* (Wartburg: 1989) p. 214.

If the dragon stole grain from others to give it to its master, then the drak would be black. According to Silesian legends, it would carry the stolen goods in the shells of nuts or eggs while flying. In its master's house, it would adopt the appearance of a chicken, referred to as an *Erdhühnchen* (in English: "earth-chicken"). In terms of its care, it was like a money demon, although as a grain demon, it would be given a colourful skirt each year.

The dragon also appeared as a butter or milk demon. In this role, it sucked the milk from cows to bring it to its master. Afterwards, the animals would give blood, rather than milk. Obtaining the butter was a more difficult process: it would often bring only one spoonful from 100 villages. The "dragon of Walterdorf" brings its owner more when, asked what it should bring, she answers: "Bring me one Nösel of milk from each house in 100 villages."

"The farmer Nijar in Zirkow had the Drak, the whole village knew that; for the creature had often been seen driving into the chimney of his house in the form of a fiery ball with a long tail of fire. One night a neighbour heard threshing going on in the Nijar's barn. 'What can that be?' he thought to himself, 'He won't let people work day and night, will he?' Because the situation seemed too strange to the neighbour, he got out of bed, went to the barn and shouted: 'A thousand! Nijar, do you thresh here all night?' He was not able to see Nijar, but there was a small, ugly fellow stand too strange to the neighbour, he got out of bed, went to the barn and shouted: 'A thousand! Nijar, do you thresh here all night?' which the dragon had threshed for him. It was easy to get filthy rich that way."

Leander Petzoldt, *Deutsche Volkssagen*, (Wiesbaden: 2007) p. 255.

It was said in Hessen that anyone seeing a drak flying by and wanting to know what it was carrying need only call: "No ferryman travels over land or bridge without leaving his toll behind." Then the dragon would be forced to drop what it was carrying. In Schleswig-Holstein and Mecklenburg-Vorpommern, it was said one should stand under a roof, expose one's backside and point it at the dragon so that, shocked, it would let everything fall. As was usual for tampering with supernatural creatures, caution was advised. If you forced a drak to drop its treasure, then you had to stand under a roof, otherwise the drak would rain down lice, feces, or any other type of filth. If this happened, it was reported that the stink would remain for the unfortunate recipient's lifetime. The message also had to be carefully chosen, as a legend from Lower Saxony tells:

"One night, between eleven and midnight, a shepherd sitting in his cart saw Stöpke crossing the sky with his long glowing tail. He called out to him, 'Half part!' The Devil asked him to leave everything he was carrying, he wanted to bring it to a child's christening, where it was truly needed. But the shepherd did not agree, and so Stöpke threw down the ham, sausage, cheese, butter, and a whole variety of dishes. A while later Stöpke passed by again and told the shepherd to call 'half part!' once more. But the shepherd replied that he still had supplies and did not need any more. On hearing this, Stöpke dropped a millstone from the air, breaking the towbar on the shepherd's cart. If the shepherd had called 'half part!' Stöpke would have dropped the heavy stone on his head, killing him."

Leander Petzoldt, *Deutsche Volkssagen*, (Wiesbaden: 2007) p. 254.

"HE HAS THE DRAGON!"—PLAYING WITH THE DEVIL

As with other household spirits, the "ownership" of a dragon brought several requirements. The dragon must be cared for, fed (with cooked food, not too hot), and its hiding place kept secret, otherwise it would fly away. Sometimes it had to be honoured with words, ceremonies, or sacrifices of milk. Where these customs were breached, it would beat anyone who failed to follow its wishes, even witches. It was also difficult to rid oneself of a dragon: "[. . .] A strange customer said that anyone who had owned a dragon was unable to die unless he had passed it on to another person with a handshake," it was said in Seitenroda, in Thüringen. In other legends it is said to be sufficient to lie on top of a dung heap—a motif which also plays a role in the demonological legend of "Der mitbegrabene Drache zu Weißenborn," the dragon of Weissenborn who was also buried.

Jiri Daschitzsky, "About a terrible and marvelous comet as appeared the Tuesday after St. Martin's Day (1577-11-12) on heaven," Woodcut, 1577, (Prague: in *Zentralbibliothek Zurich*), Wikimedia Commons.

"The grandmother of a rich farmer in Weissenborn had died. She had suffered greatly at the end, and it was only when her relatives placed some dung under her pillow that she was able to die. The coffin was blessed by the priest and then lowered into the ground. But then there came the sound of knocking and scratching. The priest wanted the gravediggers to open the coffin. The farmer, shocked, told them to quickly bury the coffin, 'The dragon is in the coffin, we are delighted he is gone!' From that time forward the house was peaceful, with none of the ghostly apparitions everyone had talked of before."

Dietrich Kühn, *Sagen und Legenden aus Thüringen*, (Wartburg: 1989), p. 215.

Wilhelm Hess, *Leaflet of a comet*, 1687, from *Himmels- und Natureerscheinungen in Einblattdrucken des XV. bis XVIII* (1911), https://commons.wikimedia.org/wiki/File:Wahre_und_eigentliche_Abbildung_eines_Entsetzlichen_Wunderzeichens.jpg#/media/File:Wahre_und_eigentliche_Abbildung_eines_Entsetzlichen_Wunderzeichens.jpg.

Although the belief in household spirits was clearly abound in Germany, there was scientific resistance to the fear of dragons. In his *Vermischte Beiträge einer nähern Einsicht in das Gesammte Geisterreich*, the educator Elias Caspar Reichard examines the phenomenon of the dragon:

"Sulfuric steam in many forms rises from the earth, mixing the flammable parts which rise into the air with the smoke. Like all the acid salts, the [. . .] vitriol acid absorbs these little particles and fire elements, creating a material which is easy to ignite [. . .] If a large quantity of this flammable essence is lit, it creates a flash which then—by rapidly expanding and violently slamming the air together—creates thunder. But when it is slowly ignited, and just a little at a time, then the substance produces the northern lights, the lightning, the sprightly children, the burning beams, the dancing goats, and the flying dragons."

Elias Caspar Reichhard, *Vermischte Beiträge einer nähern Einsicht in das Gesammte Geisterreich*, (Helmstedt: 1781).

Reichard offers a detailed description of the supposed processes behind the fiery appearance of the drak, from its creation to its entry through the chimneys of small houses. During the Enlightenment, the drak, like other apparitions, was demystified, with the natural sciences discovering explanations for similar phenomena. The fiery being, which only a few decades previously people were paying with their lives to allegedly own, kept appearing in folktales right through the early twentieth century. However, in contrast to the kobold or heinzelmännchen, today the term "house dragon" only remains as a pejorative term for domineering women.

"When a guesthouse in Seitenroda still sold bottled beer, several thirsty men wanted to buy beer late at night. And one of them insisted on helping the innkeeper with carrying up the bottles from the cellar. The innkeeper did everything he could to stop the man entering the cellar. But the man climbed down the stairs into the cellar, and halfway down he suddenly felt something fiery jumping at his neck, causing him to cry out in panic. A couple of days later the poor man died. It was said that the house dragon had frightened him to death."

Kurt Gress, *Holzlandsagen*, (Leipzig: 1870) p. 59.

> " When a guesthouse in Seitenroda still sold bottled beer, several thirsty men wanted to buy beer late at night. And one of them insisted on helping the innkeeper with carrying up the bottles from the cellar. The innkeeper did everything he could to stop the man entering the cellar. But the man climbed down the stairs into the cellar, and halfway down he suddenly felt something fiery jumping at his neck, causing him to cry out in panic. A couple of days later the poor man died. It was said that the house dragon had frightened him to death. "

Kurt Gress, *Holzlandsagen,* (Leipzig: 1870) p. 59.

Dangerous Fiery Dragon or Wet Chicken?

The drak's appearance

A POLYMORPHIC CREATURE OF FLAMES

Within the regions in which it appeared, the drak took many forms. Where the drak is synonymous with the kobold, it might appear as a small man, dressed in red. In many areas it is described as taking various animal forms: a black, fiery cat; a colourfully brindled calf; a wet or black chicken; or a three-legged hare. Usually, the drak had a fiery appearance, manifesting as a column of fire, fiery streaks, or a ball of flames. Some legends also describe a fiery "Wiesbaum," the rod attached to a loaded hay wagon which prevented the hay from falling off. It is more rarely depicted as a burning serpent with a distorted face.

Here the drak's appearance is least reminiscent of a dragon with wings or a serpent-like creature. For many people, the name "dragon" only conjures up images of a lizard-like mythical creature, and, in German-speaking regions, "house dragon" is now solely a term applied to argumentative females in the household.

"When you see long fiery streaks across the night sky, that is the Draak *or dragon in flight. One morning two servants were threshing in a barn in Grävenitz, and as it was winter it was still dark. Suddenly it became as light as day, and they noticed that the light came from the farmhouse. They hurried over, believing it was on fire. Then they heard something heavy falling into the pig's trough, and then loudly lapping, like an animal drinking. After a few moments, the fiery mass rose from the trough, and flew off through the air, without having caused any damage. They realized that it must have been a dragon who was carrying too much wheat, and so, becoming thirsty, quenched its thirst in the pig trough."*

Adalbert Kuhn, *Märkische Sagen und Märchen nebst einem Anhange von Gebräuchen und Aberglauben*, (Berlin: 1843) p. 48.

THE
DRAK

FORM

"Most fall down the chimney into the houses in the form of a fireball, releasing their treasures, milk, eggs, and money."

Ludwig Bechstein, *Deutsches Sagenbuch*, (Leipzig: 1853), p. 374.

The fireball is the basic shape for the dragon. With reference to meteorites and lava, there is a round lump of solidified rock, covered with a series of glowing veins.

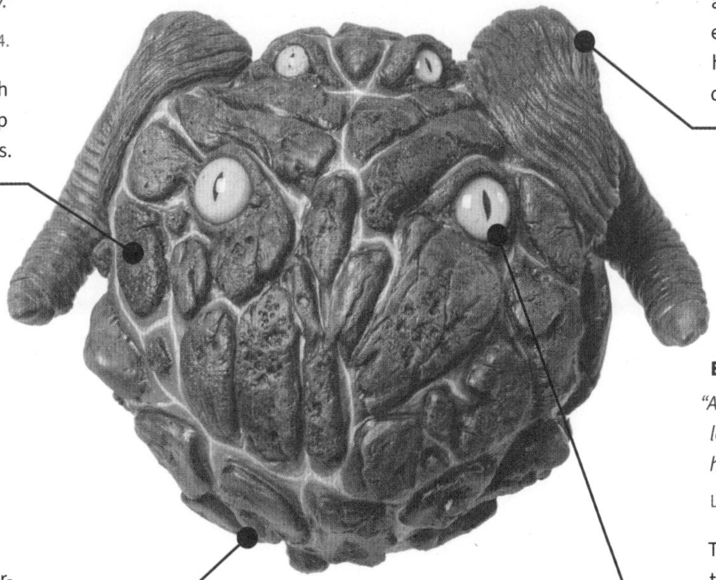

HORNS

Two, almost totally solidified horns of grey stone emanate from the fiery body. The drak was said to be an embodiment of the Devil, more so than any other household spirit. This link is highlighted by the horns, and underscores the threat posed by the flaming demon.

EYES

"A man from Döbern often saw the dragon flying by. Once, leaving his house at an early hour, the dragon flitted past him over the door, its big blue eyes staring at him."

Leander Petzoldt, *Deutsche Volkssagen,* (Wiesbaden: 2007) 254.

The light blue here matches the middle of a flame to give the drak its piercing stare. The iris is surrounded by a yellow border so that the eyes stand out from the sculpture, although fitting well into the overall colour scheme. The snake-like, pointed pupils hint at images of a serpent-like dragon. It has two pairs of eyes to highlight its otherness.

COLOUR

Containing red, yellow, and blue, the sculpture incorporates all the colours of fire. Painting the sculpture with up to ten different hues of red and yellow has given it the feeling of scorching heat, in contrast to the solidified, almost black rock.

"A schoolboy from Boblas once poked around in the wall of a cemetery. Under the firemen's ladders stored there he found a chicken. It looked at him trustingly, and so he picked it up and took it home. There he proudly placed it in the middle of the parlour. The mother looked at the animal only briefly, immediately sensing its eerie gaze. The boy was instructed to return it to where he had found it as quickly as possible, and there it disappeared before his very eyes. If they had kept it in the house, they would never have been able to get rid of it."

Dietrich Kühn, *Sagen und Legenden aus Thüringen*, (Wartburg: 1989), p. 214.

The Holzfräulein

"They are very small, have their place on the oven, on a tree stump, and are believed to be wretched souls frequently hounded, caught, and torn apart by the *Holzhetzern*. They are seldom taller than three shoes in height, their faces covered with moss, which is why they are also called little moss women, or sometimes *Hulzfral, Holzfralerl, Holzweibl.*"

From Schönwerth, *Aus der Oberpfalz, Sitten und Sagen.* Vol. 2, (1858) p. 359.

Forest Spirits in the Service of Mankind

Our ancestors imagined that the harsh natural environment, from which people were forced to wrest a living, was populated by spirits and demons. Nature's inexplicable ways were especially suited for projecting fears and desires through stories. Dark forests, deep systems of caves, and broad lakes were homes to natural spirits which were as changeable as nature itself. However, these creatures seldom stayed with their own kind: German legends tell of forest spirits who leave their sacred groves, seeking contact with humans; many came to serve as household spirits.

A HIDDEN PEOPLE

The holzfräulein, or wood women, were forest spirits which sought out human houses where they served the inhabitants. Much of the literature on the subject was penned by Schönwerth, who collected a wealth of legends and tales of the more regional hulzfral of the Oberpfalz and bordering regions.

However, "moss women" and "wood women" were known throughout the German-speaking region and beyond. They were usually considered to be mortal creatures, although with special abilities and an otherworldly connection to their groves. Some tales even go so far as to link their lives to the trees.

"Their lives are bound to those of the woodland trees. When a human twists a sapling round and round until bark and bast break, a wood woman must die."

Mannhardt, Wilhelm & Heuschkel, Walter. Wald- und Feldkulte, (Berlin: Borntraeger) 1875.

In some areas they were also believed to be poor souls searching for salvation. They were regarded as good spirits, well-disposed toward humans, and capable of rewarding those who worked hard. Their preferred location was the forest where they lived in hollow trees, under roots and rocks, or in caves. The legends include not only female wood people, but also entire families, living in secret and occasionally encountering humans.

"They live as married couples and have children. The married couples live in hollow trees, the youngsters are separated according to gender and usually live on beds of moss under shelters. At weddings, they ask humans to bake something for them, if only a little cake made of ash. When treated well, they repay their good treatment with gold. They wash their faces in the dew which gathers on the lady's mantle in the morning, baring their bodies to the dew in the meadows. They dry themselves with moss."

Mannhardt, Wilhelm & Heuschkel, Walter. Wald- und Feldkulte, (Berlin: Borntraeger) 1875.

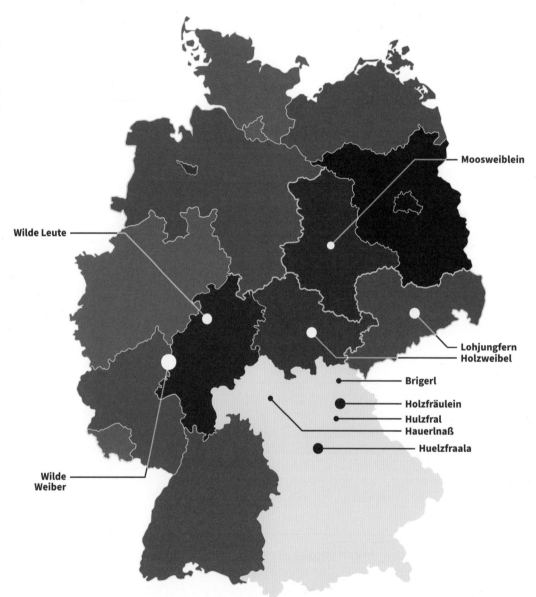

NAME VARIANTS OF THE HOLZFRÄULEIN WITHIN GERMANY

Moosweiblein

Wilde Leute

Lohjungfern
Holzweibel

Brigerl

Holzfräulein
Hulzfral
Hauerlnaß

Huelzfraala

Wilde Weiber

THE SPIRITS OF THE FORESTS

Forests hold a particular fascination for urban-dwelling humans. Germany is a country covered in lush forests and, in the absence of human activity, would be almost entirely covered by beechwoods. The beech has been the dominant tree species in Germany since the Bronze Age, so that beechwood canopy has been part of the landscape and context in the region for centuries. Historically, people did not spend time in the forest for pleasure but rather out of necessity: they were reliant on timber for fire and charcoal, toolmaking and construction, and for various utility and handicraft uses. Farmers, like travellers, had to deal with wild and dangerous animals living in the forests. The deliberate forest depletion and clearance were so extensive that as early as the eighteenth century reforestation efforts had begun in order to produce the quantities of timber needed. This period marked the start of the German forestry industry.

The image of the fairy-tale forest—a lovely and secretive place—is a by-product of the Romantic period and was particularly popular amongst the upper-middle classes and artists. Writers and poets treated forests as locations for mystical, mysterious experiences and the locale for the spirits of popular belief. Considering the nostalgic glorification sweeping the period, and the forest as a symbol of the power of nature, it is therefore unsurprising that forests play such a prominent role in nineteenth century tales and legends. Yet even before the Romantic period, people honoured the natural world and the places within it. Historical evidence suggests that the emerging Catholic Church was forced to battle a pre-Christian worship of sacred groves in Central Europe. Following the Saxon Wars, in 782 AD Charlemagne instituted the *Capitulatio de partibus Saxoniae* which forced the subdued Saxons to convert to Christianity. This law also deemed the worship of springs and trees a punishable offence.

"Whosoever makes vows to springs, trees, or sacred groves according to pagan customs, or makes sacrifices according to pagan customs and organizes a shared meal in honour of idols, must pay as a nobleman sixty, as a freeman thirty, as a bondsman fifteen sol. And if he does not have the money, he must work in the service of the Church."

Charlemagne, *Capitulatio de partibus Saxione*, (p. 782).

The issue of venerating forest spirits remained current into the high-medieval period, with the provincial synod in Trier forbidding the worship of springs and trees in 1227. However, the population stubbornly held onto many of their customs and religious beliefs. Many of the legends recorded in the nineteenth century centre

119

upon the forest creatures and trees, among them the little moss and wood women. They bear a striking similarity to the "wild women" in Hessen, the Rhineland, and Baden. Wild women were forest spirits, sometimes of giant stature, sometimes dwarf-sized, and either beautiful or profoundly ugly.

"A long time ago the wild women lived in the caves above Langenaubach. They were often seen sitting by the cave entrance where they combed their hair and sang beautiful songs. They were devoted to good and hardworking people, helping them wherever they could. On the slopes of the Fuchskaute lived a poor but honest shepherd of whom they were particularly fond. They came to him often, bringing him good bread so that he would never go hungry, and showing him the herbs to heal his sick sheep. They even helped many industrious people during harvest."

Karl Löber, *Haigerer Heft. Beitrage zur Geschichte und zum Leben der Stadt Haiger und ihres Raumes. Heft II. Saben/Vogeschichte,* (Stadt Haiger: 1972).

THE FOREST WOMAN AS A HELPFUL HOUSE SPIRIT

There are various reasons why forest spirits helped humans with their daily work and in their houses. The holzfräulein often rewarded particularly hardworking or honest people. They usually lived in the house or regularly visited it. Like kobolds, holzfräulein preferred to be positioned close to the oven, the heart of the home and the action, allowing them to observe undisturbed. This similarity may indicate a link between the forest women and ancestral spirits. They would help farmers with their duties and give advice on working the fields and keeping cattle. They were especially valued for their considerable knowledge of healing herbs and their ability to see into the future. However, many legends report a far more dramatic reason for a holzfräulein entering the human realm—in a panic-stricken flight from the Wild Hunt. As good spirits, the holzfräulein lived in permanent fear of evil, personified as *"Wildjäger"* or *"Holzhetzer"* ("wild hunters" or "agitators") which would lead a horde of evil creatures to hunt down and prey on both humans and good spirits alike.

The subject of moss people and their flight from the Wild Hunt was also known to the scholar Johannes Praetorius, who wrote about them in his 1666 *Neuen Welt-Beschreibung.* The Brothers Grimm reproduced Praetorius's descriptions in a clearer form:

"Around the year 1635, a farmer named Hans Krepel from the region around Saalfeld needed to cut down wood on the heathland in the afternoon. A little moss woman came up to him and said: 'Father, when you finish and go home for the evening, cut three crosses into the stump of the last tree you fell, and all will be well.' Having said this, she then left. The farmer, who was a rude and coarse man, thought he could ignore this type of nonsense coming from such a spirit and failed to cut three crosses into the trunk before going home in the evening. The next day he returned to the forest to continue chopping; the moss woman appeared again and said: 'Why didn't you mark the three crosses? It would have helped us both because this afternoon we will be hunted long into the night by the Wild Hunt, and we will die a miserable death and will have no peace from them, because there are no tree stumps with engraved crosses upon which we can sit, and from which they cannot take us, making us safe.'"

Grimm, Jacob & Wilhelm. *Deutsche Sagen*, (Munich: 1965), p. 691.

Schönwerth also described the Wild Hunt which swept diabolically over the land. The holzfräulein could only find salvation in a house belonging to honest people, or on tree stumps in which woodcutters had engraved three crosses.

"The wild hunters appear in great number, making a horrible din which is heard from far away. They bark like dogs and are often assumed to be dogs. They belong to the Wild Hunt, although they themselves are hunted by the Devil. Their name comes from the way in which they hunt the poor holzfräulein, to torment them. But the holzfräulein can save themselves by sitting on a tree stump into which the woodcutter has chopped three crosses after felling. This is a firm belief, and the woodcutters never fail to chop three crosses into the trunk to provide a place where the holzfräulein can rest."

Franz Schönwerth. *Aus der Oberpfalz. Sitten und Sagen*. Vol. 2, (Augsburg: 1858) p. 145 & 152.

Here we see a fascinating aspect of the holzfräulein legends: in contrast to most spirits, the relationship with Christianity is not fundamentally unilateral, but instead contradictory. The wood women are good spirits—in contrast to kobolds and dwarfs, they are not offended by pealing bells and prayer, but instead the three crosses carved into a tree stump protect them. Despite this, several legends say that wood people only ate bread over which no cross had been made while baking.

Friedrich Wilhelm Heine, *Wodan's wilde Jagd*, 1882, in *Nordisch-germanische Götter und Helden*, (Leipzig & Berlin: Otto Spamer, 1882).

Whether the holzfräulein enter houses to escape their pursuers or of their own free will, their positive nature brings humans fortune and blessings. They carry out daily chores in the house and home, scrubbing the floors, feeding and milking the cows, mowing the grass, and aiding during harvest by cutting the wheat. They demand that humans share their food in payment and require silence and harmony. Where there is argument and resentment, they leave.

During their work, the holzfräulein often mention their fear of the hunters who seek them out and wish to kill them. Consequently, reports from Thüringen of the moss people, led by the *Buschgroßmutter* (or "Shrub Grandmother"), appearing in hordes, and tearing through the country like the Wild Hunt are surprising:

"According to certain peasant tales, a demonic creature called the Buschgroß-mutter *("Shrub Grandmother") dwells near Leutenberg and on the left bank of river Saale. She has many daughters, called* Moosfräuleins *("moss ladies"), with whom she roves around the country at certain times and upon certain holy nights. It is not good to meet her, for she has wild, staring eyes and crazy, unkempt hair that often frightens people. Often, she drives around in a little cart or wagon, and at such times it is wise to stay out of her way. Children are afraid of this* Putzmommel *(hooded, female bogey) and delight in whispering tales of her to frighten each other."*

Ludwig Bechstein, *Deutsches Sagenbuch*, (Leipzig: 1853), p. 379f.

The forest spirits not only leave their traces in legend, they also survive to the current day in the names of fields, such as the Wildweiberhäuschen, Frauenhöhlen, and Waldfrauenloch, or terrain such as the Jungfernsitz and Leinwandbleiche.

THE FOREST WOMAN AS A SEDUCTRESS

In contrast to the small, motherly moss women, the larger wild women can also initiate erotic relationships with humans, even leading to marriage. They seek out married farmers in their bedrooms when their wives have left to work. The forest women are usually unaware that the men are married, at least in the alpine legends, and demand absolute faithfulness from their human partners. Forest spirits, as with most of the figures presented here, punish humans for violations of norms and prohibitions even outside a romantic relationship. Within the relationship itself there exists a taboo on speaking the moss woman's name, as well as a prohibition on asking about her origins.

When insulted by humans, the moss women disappear forever. These tales of *Mahrtenehen*—marriages between humans and mythical beings—are clearly stories of adultery, reflecting the wishes and desires of wanting to break free from Christian moral and social conventions.

MAHRTENEHE—MARRIAGE TO A SPIRIT

The *Mahrtenehe* is the erotic, sexually motivated love affair or marriage of a (usually) male human to a supernatural being. It lasts until a specific ban or taboo is violated, at which point the relationship ends.

"There lived in Beschen a farmer who had married a forest woman. At his wedding he had been required to promise his wife never to scold her, otherwise she would disappear. They lived together happily and peacefully for a long time. But once, just before the harvest, while the farmer was away, driving to Vienna on his wagon, his wife went into the fields, cut down the green wheat and carried it all home [. . .] On hearing this, the farmer began to rant and rail against his wife. He drove home in a rage. But his wife was already gone. A dreadful storm broke and the hail destroyed all the crops in the fields; however, the farmer's green wheat was fully ripe and good. And then he realized that his wife had predicted the storm, and so had saved the wheat. He mourned her loss greatly, but she was gone and never returned."

Josef Virgil Grohmann, *Sagen-Buch von Böhmen und Mähren*. Vol. 1, (Prague: 1863) p. 130.

The Old Woman and the Forest

The holzfräulein's appearance

GREEN HAIR AND GREY CLOTHES

As with almost all legendary figures in German folklore, there are many different descriptions of the holzfräulein. Some tell of an old, tiny woman of human physique, while others describe her as having skin as cracked as tree bark with hair like moss. The moss woman's clothing can vary as much as her appearance. If not wearing moss, then they are described as ragged or even naked. The fabric they wore was mostly rough and worn, and grey or faded in colour.

In interpreting her appearance an emphasis was given to the holzfräulein's age and wisdom, as well as her otherworldly nature. It was particularly important that her eyes and facial expressions lend her gravitas. Therefore, two different models were created to highlight the vast differences in characteristics offered by the texts studied. They are based on two legends about holzfräuleins: the *Holzfralla* of Upper Franconia, and the *Buschweibchen* of today's Czech Republic.

THE **HOLZFRALLA** OF **UPPER FRANCONIA**

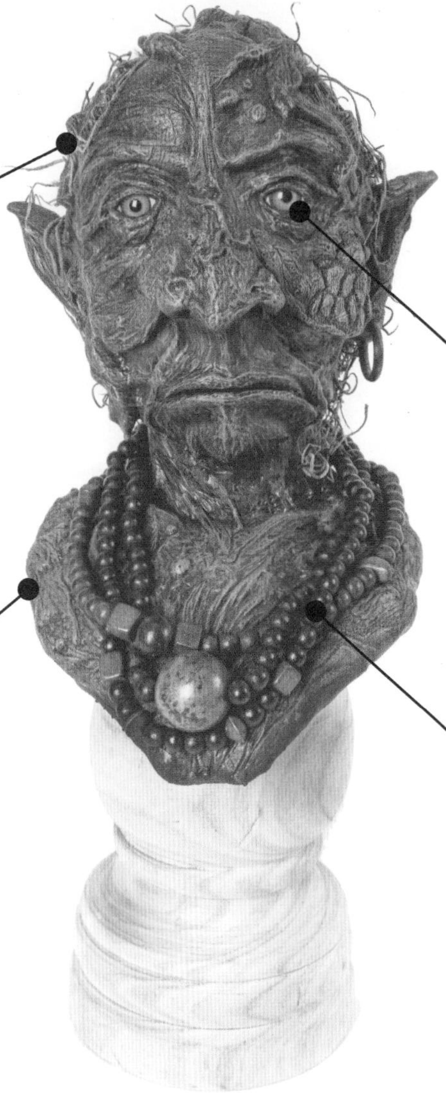

HAIR

Legends tell of thin hair composed entirely of moss. Here, in addition to preserved moss, artificial moss was used to ensure the durability of the figures.

SKIN

"The Holzfralla is a dwarf-like female, with face and hands as grey and fissured as the bark of a fir, and with hair and clothes of moss."

G Heinz, *Die Sage vom Oberfränkischen Holzfräulein,* (Frankenwald: 1926) p. 15–16.

While wild women are often described as stunningly beautiful with silver hair, moss women and holzfräuleins are wrinkled and gnarled figures whose age and experience are clearly written in their faces. The dark and deeply furrowed woody skin is reminiscent of bark.

EYES

The blue, human eyes stand in contrast to the dark skin. Slightly squinting, the holzfralla stares past the observer, into their future.

WOODEN JEWELLERY

The holzfralla's jewellery—necklaces and earrings—is made from natural materials such as wood and stones.

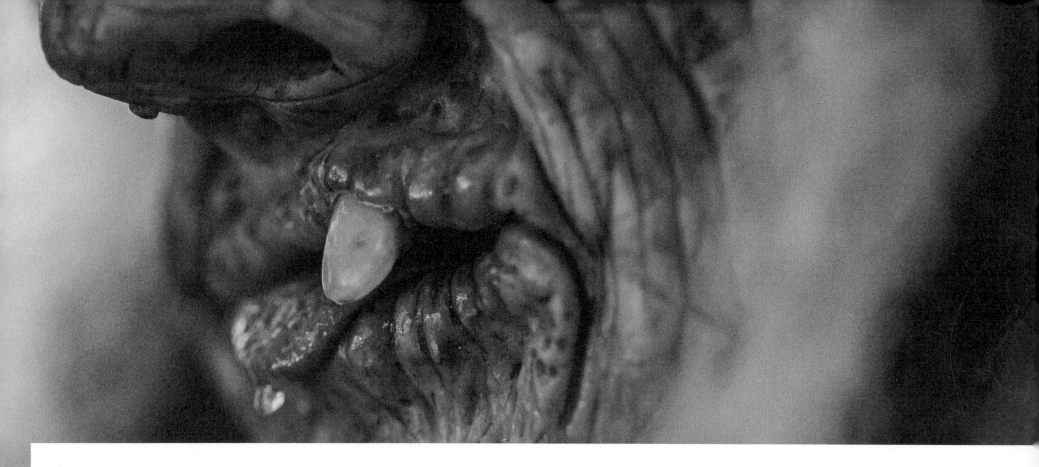

THE BUSCHWEIBCHEN OF THE BOHEMIAN FORESTS

The appearance of the buschweibchen, or shrub woman, is interpreted according to the description taken from Grohmann's collection of legends, with supplementary details drawn from other legends. The stooped posture, long white hair, and knobby stick are recreated from Bohemian legends.

Her persecution by the hordes of the Wild Hunt is also clear: they have left the buschweibchen blind in one eye and with a deep scar. Just like the holzfräulein and moss women, these spirits were also described as wise, and that wisdom brought humans' prosperity or assistance in times of need. It was even said some could tell fortunes.

"*The* buschweiblein *lives in the depths of the forest, only allowing itself to be seen once in a century. When I was still a young girl, I often drove the priest's cows to the meadow [. . .] Once there was a rustling in the shrubbery and out stepped an old woman, the sight of whom was slightly frightening. I was soon convinced it must be the* buschweiblein, *because she looked just like my grandmother had described her: an old, stooping woman, with long, snow-white, wild-looking hair. She held a knotty stick in her hand; her apron was tied as though carrying something within; and moss grew on her feet.*"

Adalbert Kuhn, *Märkische Sagen und Märchen nebst einem Anhange von Gebräuchen und Aberglauben,* (Berlin: 1843) p. 48–49.

THE **SHRUBWOMAN** OF THE **BOHEMIAN FORESTS**

STAFF

"As they are knowledgeable about the power of nature and give medical advice, they are also wise women."

Franz Schönwerth. *Aus der Oberpfalz. Sitten und Sagen.* Vol. 2, (Augsburg: 1858), p. 361.

The winding staff is decorated with wooden pearls and natural materials, it supports the forest spirit with her faltering gait. It underscores her wisdom and is a traditional sign of magical power which the holzfräulein was believed to possess.

HAIR

"Her hair was long and snow white, hanging in wild disorder around her head."

Josef Virgil Grohmann, *Sagen-Buch von Böhmen und Mähren.* Vol. 1, (Prague: 1863) p. 132.

Moss women have hair which is long, wild in appearance, and snow white in colour, although occasionally it could be black or yellow.

SKIN

"The holzfräulein are real people with old faces, and rough, wrinkled skin."

Roland Röhrich, Franz Xaver Schönwerth: *Leben und Werk,* (Lass-leben: 1975) p. 69, no. 108.

BASKET

"They carry baskets made from unstripped willow on their back."

Ludwig Bechstein, *Thüringer Sagenbuch,* (Vienna & Leipzig: 1858) p. 80.

Sometimes they carried a bundle of wood in the basket on their back, or brushwood in their aprons. These baskets, worn like a rucksack, were made from unstripped willow.

FACE

"The right eye is black and positioned lower than the right."

Josef Virgil Grohmann, *Sagen-Buch von Böhmen und Mähren.* Vol. 1, (Prague: 1863) p. 123.

The hordes of the Wild Hunt chased the forest women. The *Buschweiblein* is blind in one eye, the outcome of an encounter with the Hunt.

"While they slept, a hunchbacked, half-blind moss woman crept past."

Leander Petzoldt, *Deutsche Volkssagen,* (Wiesbaden: 2007) p. 185.

CLOTHES

"They were grey in appearance, with faces covered in moss, old grey clothing, and were very small."

Ludwig Bechstein, *Deutsches Sagenbuch,* (Leipzig: 1853), p. 80.

> "Whenever a cake was baked in Bärnau, or dumplings made, the farmer's wife was never allowed to count what was in the pan, so that the holzfräulein could have her share; they also ate the crusts of bread over which no cross had been made before baking, so called unblessed bread."

Franz Schönwerth, *Aus der Oberpfalz. Sitten und Sagen.* Vol. 2, (Augsburg: 1858), p. 360.

The Geldmännlein

Thereupon one takes them in the house, washes them clean in red wine, wraps them in a white and red silk cloth, lays them in a wooden casket, washes them every Friday, and gives them a new white shirt on every new moon. When one calls the alraun it answers, revealing future and secret things which lead to welfare and prosperity. From that time onwards the owner has no more enemies, can never be poor, and, if he has no children, the marriage will then be fertile. A coin placed next to it at night has been doubled by the morning; if the owner wishes to maintain its service for a long time, and ensure it neither leaves nor dies, then they are careful not to overload it; a half a Thaler could be placed next to it every night, but never more than a ducat, and not always, just occasionally.

Grimm, Jacob & Wilhelm. *Deutsche Sagen*, (Munich: 1965), p. 691.

A Devilish Root Brings Wealth

In the seventeenth century, if someone became suddenly rich without an easy explanation, then they were often said to possess a geldmännlein, or "small money man." This small, human-like household spirit brought its owner money, duplicated coins, or even produced them by itself. They were usually kept in a special place, such as over the fireplace, or in a box under the bed.

ON BREEDERS OF MONEY AND DEFECATORS OF DUCATS

The term "geldmännlein" is first documented in 1657, when Caspar Michel Fuchs from Sulzfeld near Meiningen was accused of owning a spirit that created money. Just like other household spirits, the geldmännlein is known by many names, although nowhere else is this divergence in terminology so difficult to explain. The money-spinning creature is a perfect example of the convoluted and long process of oral history, retellings, and contamination of those stories which all make this creature's origins difficult to retrace today.

Historical sources report that the terms "alraun(e)," "mandrake," and *Heck(emännchen)* are often used synonymously, sometimes to describe separate but similar beings, and sometimes—in individual lexicological entries—as different creatures but with shared characteristics. Whether the term "alraun/mandrake" is used as a synonym for geldmännlein, or whether the geldmännlein were just strongly associated with a belief in mandrakes was simply not addressed until now. The same applies to the *Heckmännchen* which the dictionary of German folklore describes as follows:

"In folklore the Heckmännchen *is a small kobold which brings or breeds money or is made from gold and grows."*

Oswald Erich & Richard Beitl, *Wörterbuch der deutschen Volkskunde*, (Leipzig: 1936).

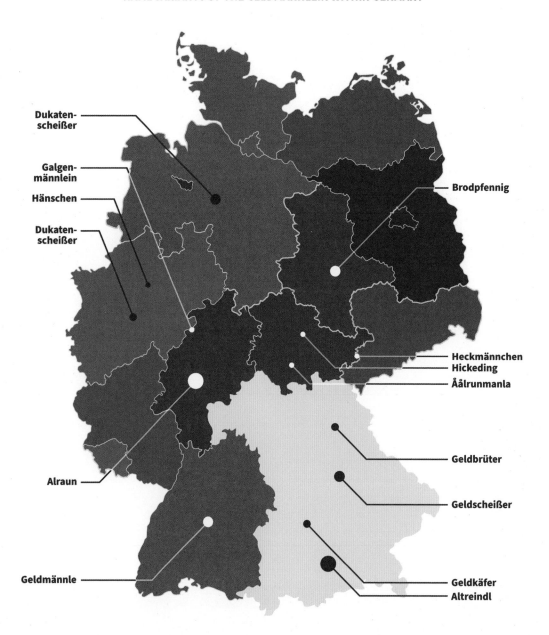

NAME VARIANTS OF THE GELDMÄNNLEIN WITHIN GERMANY

Dukaten-scheißer
Galgen-männlein
Hänschen
Dukaten-scheißer
Brodpfennig
Heckmännchen
Hickeding
Åålrunmanla
Alraun
Geldbrüter
Geldscheißer
Geldmännle
Geldkäfer
Altreindl

The term "heckmännchen" is therefore a regional expression for a helpful household spirit in Central Germany. What is interesting here is its connection with the kobold and drak: the kobold as a helpful household spirit and the drak as a money demon. Heckmännchen, then, is not a legendary figure itself, but rather a type of geldmännlein. In Silesia, the geldmännlein is known as a spiritus, indicating a relationship with the *spiritus familiaris*—the hybrid creature, part spider, part scorpion, we have already met. The "little gold-breeding man" is also the origin of the *Heck(e)taler*, said to arise when an alraun is kept in a casket for a year and a day: when the casket is opened, a taler—a so-called *Hecktaler*—is found lying next to the alraun. The hecktaler follows its owner forever. When used to pay for something, it would quickly find its way back from the seller's cash box into its owner's pocket.

"The root of the plant previously described (mandrake) is carved into a house spirit; used in a diminutive form, the Alraunchen. *This root is white, thick, the lower part split into two, like two crossed human legs, and with thin fibres, as if covered with hair; with human features but miniature in form [. . .] Such house spirits are known in some places as* Galgenmännchen *because the roots of the mandrake are said to grow under the gallows (Galgen—gallows);* Heinzelmännchen; Glücksmännchen; Erdmännchen; Geldmännchen, *because it brings money;* Herenmännchen; *and in Lower Saxony* Alruniken. *As true mandrake root is so rare in Germany, the roots of the bryony (Bryonia, L.), externally similar in appearance, are often sold as mandrake [. . .]"*

Johann Christoph Adelung, *Grammatisch-kritisches Wörterbuch der Hochdeutschen Mundart*, (Vienna: 1811) p. 226.

Thus, the geldmännlein and alraun follow the same narrative and the same basic history. However, the functions and abilities of the alraun far outstrip those of the household spirit, as in addition to its household spirit abilities it is also a rare magical plant with a range of uses. The geldmännlein are therefore a type of *mandrake*, but the *mandrake* does not always fulfill the role of the geldmännlein.

SHORT CULTURAL HISTORY OF THE MANDRAKE

The sinister reputation of the alraun, or mandrake, spread over thousands of years in the tales of Asian and European peoples. It was expensive and used for healing, as a magical ingredient, and an intoxicant. Biologically, the references are usually to the same plant, *Mandragora officinarum*, a member of the nightshade family which also includes deadly nightshade and thornapples. With an often deeply split tap root which can reach forty cm down into the soil, the mandrake was frequently interpreted as having a human-like form, making it a symbol of mythical beings acting in secret. The perennial plant is widely spread throughout Southern Europe, but its increasing popularity led to it quickly being cultivated north of the Alps. The highly poisonous alkaloids it contains have an analgesic and some-what hallucinogenic effect, explaining its use as both an aphrodisiac and a narcotic.

Over time, the term "alraun(e)" was used to cover a variety of succulent roots which were carved into human-like figures for magical purposes. Its mystical and some-times sinister history is captured in a range of art and literature, the scope of which is difficult to comprehend today. The oldest reports of human-like roots date back to Assyria in the fifteenth and fourteenth centuries BC, and reports of Mardum-Giâ, the "human herb"; or Mer-e-giah, the "love plant" in Persia; while the English term "mandrake" could be a folk-etymological form of mandragora. Even Heinrich Heine (1797 – 1856) included the alraun in his poem *Waldeinsamkeit*.

"The cleverest woodland spirits are the Alraunen,
Long-bearded men with short legs,
A finger-long race of elderly men.
Where they come from, no one really knows."
Heinrich Heine, *Romanzero, Book Two, Lamentations,* (Hamburg: 1851) p. 119 ff.

The German term "alraun(e)" probably originates from the Old High German *alrûna*, with *rûna* meaning "bearer of secrets." Both the masculine New High German form alraun and feminine alraune have been in use since the fifteenth century. Although the magical plant was first cultivated in Egypt after 1600 BC, it is present in many graphic depictions. Contemporary texts report that it was used to intoxicate ene-mies to conquer them. Indications of "celebrations of the sleeping potion" also suggest a cult-like use of the alraun in religious practice. For centuries, the plant enjoyed a role in medicine, as an anesthetic used in major operations. However, the alraun is most famous as an aphrodisiac, which is first indicated in the Book of Genesis, in which mandrakes are described:

"During wheat harvest, Reuben went out into the fields and found some mandrake plants, which he brought to his mother Leah. Rachel said to Leah, 'Please give me some of your son's mandrakes.' But she said to her, 'Wasn't it enough that you took away my husband? Will you take my son's mandrakes too?' 'Very well,' Rachel said, 'he can sleep with you tonight in return for your son's mandrakes.' So when Jacob came in from the fields that evening, Leah went out to meet him. You must sleep with me, she said. I have hired you with my son's mandrakes. So he slept with her that night"
(Genesis 30:14-16).

There is also a reference to mandrakes in the explicit context of sexual intercourse in the Song of Songs. Dating back to antiquity, mandrake's stimulating effect made it a popular ingredient in love potions. The plant was also extensively used for gynecological purposes during that time, with midwives using them to increase sexual desire, encourage fertility and conception, for easing birth, as an anesthetic during Caesarian sections, as well as for killing fetuses and ending unwanted pregnancies.

The mixture of human-like appearance of the root and the physiological con-sequence of its consumption explains the mandrake's significant role in stories and legends. Where mandrakes were unavailable, they were substituted with belladonna, scopolia, or bryony, which had similar effects. Non-poisonous plants such as wild orchids were also sold as mandrakes to those willing to pay. As well as an aphrodisiac and sleeping drought, the mandrake was also a much honoured household spirit, leading to the development of a special cult associated with the plant, particularly during the medieval period.

THE MANDRAKE HARVEST

If ancient and medieval scripts are to be believed, it was not easy to procure a mandrake. The Greek philosopher Theophrastos von Eresos (371 – 287 BC) recommended holding a sword and marching around the plant three times prior to digging it up while facing west and accompanied by a second person dancing in a circle and speaking of love. The Jewish/Roman chronicler Josephus Flavius (37 – 93 AD) even warned that the root should not be pulled from the ground, as its scream was deadly. He demonstrated the process using a black dog. Flavius provides a range of guidelines for how to correctly protect one's ears to withstand the magical and deadly scream. We also find traces of belief in the mandrake in folk legends:

"It is a well-known tradition near Magdeburg, that when a man who is a thief by inheritance [. . .] or whose mother has committed a theft, or been possessed with an intense longing to steal something at the time immediately preceding his birth; it is the tradition that if such a man should be hanged, at the foot of the gallows whereon his last breath was exhaled will spring up a plant of hideous form known as the alraun or the little gallows man. It is an unsightly object to look at, and has broad, dark green leaves, with a single yellow flower. It is a feat full of the greatest danger to obtain it [. . .] The moment the earth is struck with the spade, the bitterest cries and shrieks burst forth from it, and while the roots are being laid bare demons are heard to howl in horrid concert [. . .] There is, however, happily, only one day in the month, the first Friday, on which this plant appears, and on the night of that day only may it be plucked from its hiding place [. . .] At midnight he takes his stand under the gallows, and there stuffs his ears with wool or wax, so that he may hear nothing. As the dread hour arrives, he stoops down and makes three crosses over the alraun, and then commences to dig for the roots in a perfect circle around it. When he has laid it entirely bare, so that it only holds to the ground by the points of its roots, he calls the hound to him, and ties the plant to its tail. He then shows the dog some meat, which he flings to a short distance from the spot. Ravenous with hunger, the hound springs after it, dragging the plant up by the root, but before he can reach the tempting morsel he is struck dead as by some invisible hand."

Julie Barkley & Nannette Lewis, eds., "Folk-Lore and Legends," (Germany: 2008), Gutenberg.

Historians assume that the general motif of the mandrake legends is based in early Persian and Biblical legends, as well as ancient Persian mythology. In Near Eastern myths, sperm and urine were probably linked to medieval European belief in the magical properties of plants on a gallows hill, and of a corpse's various parts. The view that the mandrake, which grows under the gallows, is the product of the sperm or urine of a thief who has been hung can be traced back to the fifteenth or sixteenth century and is also the origin of the terms "*Galgenmännchen,*" or "little gallows man" and the "geldmännlein," or "little money man."

GOOD BUSINESS AND WITCHCRAFT TRIALS

The geldmännlein ensured that business was lucrative and, when treated properly, promised its owner protection, good fortune, money, victory, and good health. However, digging up the root was a complicated procedure. Some of the legends of the mandrake were directly adopted by those of the geldmännlein. It can be assumed that proprietors of this magical root spread these tales to drive up the price. A true mandrake root would have to be imported from France or Italy at great cost, as none grew north of the Alps. As a result, figures were often carved from bryony, galangal, or alpine leeks. To make a geldmännlein appear even more realistic, they were decorated with sprouting grains of barley to represent body hair, from beard

to pubic. Records going back to the first half of the nineteenth century indicate that some of these figures were filled with a substance which was then ignited, so that it appeared to defecate coins as it burned away. This gave rise to the name *Dukatenscheißer*, "ducat shitter." This was the origin of the popular German saying *"einen Geldscheißer zu haben,"* or "having a ducat shitter," for which there are written records dating back to the first half of the nineteenth century.

The fraudulent sellers included travelling folk, jugglers, apothecaries, and alchemists, and particularly executioners who had direct access to the gallows where the plant was said to grow. As early as the thirteenth century, enlightened voices spoke out against popular belief in the geldmännlein and *Galgenmännchen*. The spirits were also a thorn in the side of the Church: from the fifteenth century onwards, many witchcraft trials involved those suspected of owning a geldmännlein, as well as a drak. The strong action taken by the Church against the trade in the mandrake, and the associated customs which it deemed superstitious practices, is therefore unsurprising. Right into the seventeenth century, the records of witchcraft trials show many accusations based on the possession or use of mandrakes. On 18 November 1726, a sealed package and a letter were found in the sacristy of the St. Blasii Church in Nordhausen, Thüringen. The package allegedly

Witch with familiars, ~ 1579, (digitalized and revised, 2012), Wikimedia Commons.

contained a *Heckmännchen*, while the letter instructed the local priest to warn all Christians against such devilish beings. Despite the many trials, the trade in the money-producing root continued. Around 1900, the price reached up to sixty taler. The carved roots continued to be sold for their magical aphrodisiac and fertility properties and to bring fortune and riches right up to the early twentieth century.

CORRECT CARE AND MAINTENANCE

If, having overcome all the obstacles, someone had managed to acquire a geldmännlein, then the correct care was needed if the owner's wealth was to be multiplied. The new household spirit had to be regularly bathed in wine and/or water, it had to be given new clothes at each new moon, and regular ritual offerings of milk and bread. Bathing the household spirit in milk was another common practice:

"Head, torso, and fibrous limbs are crudely shaped, as well as eyes, an ugly wide mouth, and a squashed nose in a grotesque face. Every month, under a waxing moon, the rough-haired, shrivelled thing is bathed. If the bath is forgotten, it is said to whine and scream like a small child until finally bathed."
Martin Beck, *Eine Zauberwurzel. Kulturgeschichtliche Skizze*, (Leipzig: 1893).

RISKS AND SIDE EFFECTS

"Anyone who owns such a little man has pleasure and enjoyment and all the gold in the world for as long as they live, but if the owner dies without having first passed on the dreadful little man to someone else, which is only possible when it is sold for somewhat less than the owner paid for it, then their soul belongs to the Devil. Mine cost ten ducats, give me nine and it is yours. I came into possession of this dangerous good against my will, having bought it from a fraudster as a natural rarity."
From Johann Andreas Christian Löhr (1819): *Das Buch der Maehrchen für Kindheit und Jugend, nebst etzlichen Schnaken und Schnurren, anmuthig und lehrhaftig.* Vol. 1, Leipzig, p. 250.

In contrast to the magical plant, as a household spirit the geldmännlein was evil through and through. What first appears as a helpful creature cannot be simply given away. Like the *spiritus familiaris*, the owner of a geldmännlein must sell it during his own lifetime, for a price less than that which he himself paid. If he fails

to do so, his soul belongs to the Devil, and he will go to Hell when he dies. Some legends also tell of the *Galgenmännlein* who may only be sold twice or three times before their owner is doomed.

"There are also those who claim that the Gäldschyßer *was a root with the exact appearance of a little man, or was a real, living, coin-sized man. It was said he was hard to get rid of once in your possession, and when it came to its third owner, they were ruined and inescapably victims of the Devil. Every day the owner would place a coin under him, and it would then duplicate it."*
From Josef Müller (1926): *Sagen aus Uri 1–3.* Vol. 1, Basel, p. 250f.

The legends often focussed on the fear felt by an owner of a geldmännlein who was coming to the end of their life. Unable to rid themselves of the spirit, they sought desperately for alternative escapes. This often led them into the arms of the clergy.

"A farmer had an Alrünli, *that is an animal like a frog; it had made him rich. But at the end of his life he became fearful; because if he failed to rid himself of it before dying, he would go to the Devil. So he went to a Capuchin monk, wailing and complaining. The monk read him the texts and said there was nothing he could do. But then he suggested a solution. The farmer should carry the* Alrünli *to a far corner of his land, still on his property, and leave it there, and when a dog sniffs, snaps, and chases it away, then he would be saved."*
From Josef Müller (1926): *Sagen aus Uri 1–3.* Vol. 1, Basel, p. 249.

Looks Like a Weed

The geldmännlein's appearance

"In 1595, when I was still a judge, amongst the confiscated documents of an accused licentiate I came across not only a book of magic, filled with wondrous characters and sketches, but also a little casket in the shape of a coffin, in which lay an old, black little alraun man, with very long hair but no beard, used for magical purposes and to multiply gold. I tore the arm off the alraun. Those who saw this said my action would bring me misfortune at home. But I laughed, and said, those who fear such things can leave. Finally, I threw the book, casket and little man in the fire, and the only odour I could smell was that of burned root."

Kuhn, *Adalbert Märkische Sagen und Märchen nebst einem Anhange von Gebräuchen und Aberglauben*, (Berlin: 1843), p. 48.

In 1599 the Spanish Jesuit Martin Anton Delrio (1551 – 1608) published the first part of his work *Disquisitionum magicarum* which was based on the *Malleus Maleficarum* and other treatises on witches. His compendium offers a comprehensive portrayal of witchcraft and Satanism, including the geldmännlein. According to Delrio, the belief in supernatural beings, their influence on people, and the need for exorcisms was an important part of Christian teaching. His three-volume work was designed as a handbook for judges. He supplemented the descriptions of typical acts of witchcraft with "real" examples, although he sourced the majority from the works of his predecessors.

Like Delrio, in most historical sources the descriptions of the geldmännlein range from a root with a human-like form to a little man with the features of a root vegetable. Some legends offer significant variations on this theme, and the ubiquitous contamination with other figures of legend did the rest: sometimes the geldmännlein appears not only as a root of other plants, but also as a black worm, a little grey man with light-coloured eyes, or even in the form of an animal—a toad, a toad-like creature, or more rarely a black chicken (similar to the drak). In interpreting the appearance of the geldmännlein, I have drawn on the 1599 description in the *Disquisitionum Magicarum*, creating one version with "long hair" in a coffin-shaped casket, and another as the proverbial "ducat shitter" filling a treasure chest.

THE GELDMÄNNLEIN

PHYSICAL SIZE

"He opened it and shook out a finger-length, root-like figure. Without thinking any further, he put everything in his pocket."

Dietrich Kühn, *Sagen und Legenden aus Thüringen,* (Wartburg: 1989), p. 211f.

There is little specific information about the size of a geldmännlein. It is usually described as small and looking like a root, but no measurements are given. Our figure here is seventeen cm in height.

PHYSIOGNOMY

"Head, torso, and fibrous limbs are crudely shaped; as well as eyes, an ugly, wide mouth; and a squashed nose in a grotesque face."

Martin Beck, *Eine Zauberwurzel. Kulturgeschichtliche Skizze,* (Leipzig: 1893).

In interpreting its appearance, I decided to give the geldmännlein bright yellow eyes, and to focus on the grotesque face. The creature has a piercing stare and, apart from the basic features, its face is only remotely human.

SKIN & HAIR

"An old, black little alraun man [. . .] with very long hair but no beard."

Martin Anton Delrio, *Disquisitionum magicarum, Part 1,* (Louvain: 1599).

Fine roots or human hair? It is quite likely that people simply referred to the fine roots on the alraun as hair. The leaves protruding from its head also hint at hair. Whether they thought the little figure had real hair or not is difficult to say, and so here the geldmännlein has dark, almost human-like hair, and the second one has leaves, to portray both possibilities.

SEX

"The Gäldschyßer *was said to be a root with the exact appearance of a little man."*

Josef Müller, *Sagen aus Uri 1–3.* Vol. 1, (Basel: 1926) p. 250–251.

Many illustrations indicate that alraun were assumed to have different sexes, but the legends usually speak of a "little man." For that reason, sex and gender have deliberately been omitted from these two geldmännlein.

ON DARK WINGS AND SOFT PAWS

"In olden times, some farms had their own protective spirit that always made itself known when disaster threatened. It warned the people in good time and was often able to ward off the approaching disaster at the very last minute [. . .] There was one, for example, which would cluck like a sitting hen to make itself known. It always appeared to come out of the earth, and because of the clucking noise it made was called the 'earth hen.'"

Erich Hupfauf, *Hifalan Und Hafalan*, (Berenkamp: 1995) p. 57f.

Household spirits often appeared in animal form. Kobolds were known to take on the shape of a cat, calf, or dog. These spirit animals were usually black, with flaming red eyes. The legends also tell of other forms, including three-legged hares, ravens, insects, or even worms. Dwarfs and other mountain spirits could appear as rats. The fiery drak might look like a wet, black chicken, and the geldmännlein often took on the form of a toad or other toad-like being. Even snakes, such as the grass snake that could often be seen near human habitation, were often believed to be protective household spirits.

Chapter 3

Wrapping Up— Insights from Historical Research

By their very nature, spirits are difficult to grasp, making a successful "hunt" for these creatures only possible with a talented, interdisciplinary team. How could a single person ever accumulate all the know-how needed to understand such supernatural creatures? A whole series of scientific disciplines and a variety of perspectives are involved in researching spirits. These creatures and their mythos pave the way for contemporary audiences to become acquainted with and understand inexplicable phenomena, whether they belong to the past or the present.

SIX EXPERTS OFFER EXPERTISE:

Archaeologist **Tobias Janouschek** from the Colombischlössle Archaeological Museum in Freiburg reveals how household deities were honoured during the Roman Empire. He reports on the *lares* and *penates*, terms which the monk Notker Labeo would later introduce into the German language.

Tobias Gärtner, Professor of Medieval and Modern Archaeology at the Martin Luther University in Halle-Wittenberg, offers archaeological evidence for the belief in household spirits. Drawing on written sources and medieval building sacrifices, he offers a picture of early beliefs in supernatural powers in the house.

Rudolf Simek, Professor and Chair of Ancient German and Nordic Studies at the University of Bonn, offers a broader perspective with his paper on trolls, mythical beings of Scandinavian folklore. House trolls in Denmark bear a marked resemblance to German wichtel.

Burkhard Kling, art historian and Director of the Brüder Grimm Haus Museum in Steinau an der Straße, looks at the spirits in the work of the famous Brothers Grimm. They published not only legends and tales originating in the German-speaking regions, but also Irish tales of elves.

Folklorist **Janin Pisarek** brings us back to the German-speaking region in her paper which examines the phenomenon of changelings, a creature described as incorporating the dual aspects of disease and mythological transfiguration.

We end with **Eberhard Bauer** from the Institute for Frontier Areas of Psychology and Mental Health (IGPP) in Freiburg. He works with people who report inexplicable experiences, and his contribution provides an insight into investigations into modern ghostly apparitions.

Of *Lares* and *Penates*—
Honouring Household Deities in the Roman Empire

Tobias Janouschek

The pre-Roman population of Central Europe would certainly have had their own religious beliefs, not only with respect to their gods, but also spirits within the household. Yet today we have almost no understanding of these beliefs. Much of what we read today about the Celtic and Germanic religions comes from later sources, usually medieval monks who studied almost extinct religions. Our knowledge of the Celtic religions comes from Ireland, while the primary sources of information about Germanic beliefs are from Iceland. The Roman deities and their histories are thousands of years and thousands of kilometres away from the prehistoric faiths of the Germanic peoples.

All the other sources that discuss ancient religion are Roman and Greek. The Romans were the first to leave written records of any significant volume in Central Europe which allow us to explore the beliefs of those ancient peoples. During this period almost no distinction was drawn between popular belief and actual religion. Today, however, the Latin term "*superstitio*," or superstition, has come to mean a greatly exaggerated belief, with excessive immersion in ritual acts and beliefs in deities.

Roman religion was not focussed on "belief"; people imagined the gods to be truly present in everything that surrounded them. Accordingly, Roman religion was not conditional on a belief in the gods or the specific actions of an individual, but instead demanded the correct performance of ritual acts. The fundamental rule was *do ut des*, or "I give so that you might give." It is a mercantile principle: the gods keep the world running, for which humans pay in the form of required actions, usually ritual sacrifices. These rituals were also performed as a means of asking large or small favours of the gods. People would sacrifice to a goddess of healing, for example, offering small sheets of precious metal engraved with an image of the affected body part.

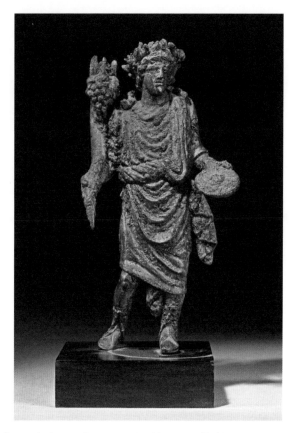

Bronze figure of a dancing *lar*, crowned with leaves and holding a cornucopia and dish. The statue measures just twenty-two cm in height. Such figures are found throughout the Roman Empire and in a variety of sizes.

Another example is offered by the consecration inscriptions which frequently include the initials V.S.L.M., an abbreviation of *votum solvit libens merito*, or "discharges the vow freely, as is deserved." This refers to the promise made to erect a votive offering bearing this inscription in gratitude for a specific service provided by a specific deity.

It is also important to distinguish between Republican and pre-Republican religion, as well as that of the later Roman Empire, for during the late Republican period—the last centuries before the birth of Christ—Roman culture was significantly exposed to Hellenistic influences. This explains the temple architecture, ritual practices, and parallels between many Roman and Greek gods which we recognize today, and especially depictions of the gods in human form. The many local deities which are personifications of places, regions, activities, or even behaviours, are evidence of original Roman beliefs, although these deities have their origins in a Celtic past; those from German-speaking regions include Abnoba, goddess of the Black Forest, and Meduna, goddess of a spring in Bad Bertrich. These types of deities could be so specific that they even failed to merit their own name: they include the—admittedly probably only jokingly—invoked gods of gambling, named in an invitation to a feast in Windisch, in Switzerland.

As well as the gods themselves, there were *Genii* (singular, *Genius*), originally ancestral spirits which served as personal protective spirits. As a result of invocations to a personal protective spirit, over time the term transformed to become an expression of that individual's personality. Analog to the specialized gods, the principle of the *Genius* was soon transferred to collectives and places, and, like the other gods, the *Genius* clearly linked the natural world with conscious entities tasked with ensuring the function of their area of responsibility. However, they only fulfilled this function sufficiently when suitably worshipped. It was also possible to purchase their favour and specific courtesies, but also to court trouble by failing to show adequate veneration. The peculiarity of this type of religion, and a reason for this long introduction, is the fluid transition from actual gods to beings which would today be described as kobolds, fairies, or natural spirits.

The oldest Roman form of such spirits and deities are the *lares*. These beings were first named in the fifth century BC, during the early days of the Republic. In addition to the official "state" gods, the *lares* were worshipped in private, until this was forbidden in the fifth century AD following Christianization. The question of the *lares*' origin was one that writers of antiquity themselves discussed. There was a theory that the *lares*, like the *Genii*, were originally the idolized spirits of the dead. This was supported by the bond between a *lar* and a single family, one which remained even when the family moved residence. However, one could argue against this

theory by highlighting that the existence of the *lares* extended far beyond houses and families—as *lares* loci, a *lar* bound to a specific place; as *lares* competi, the *lar* of a crossroads; the *lares Publici*, the *lares* of an entire locality; and even the *lares* compitales, the *lares* of entire cities in Central Italy. During the Republic, the farming population had *lares* who served as protective spirits for a piece of land, so that the origin and function of the *lares* were very similar to those of the *Genii*. However, the primary function of a *lar* was to protect, while in later times a *Genius* became a the divine power present in every human and personified within a specific person, place, or object.

As protective spirits of a family and home, during the time of the Roman Empire the *lares* were worshipped at small household altars, the *Lararia*, often together with other deities with whom the worshipper had a certain affinity, such as Mars for soldiers. Following an Augustinian reform, they always appeared in pairs, usually together with the *Genius* of the head of the household, and, in politically ambitious families, the *Genius* of the Emperor.

Patricio Lorente, *Lararium*, photograph, (2018), Wikimedia Commons.

This is *Lararium* from the Casa dei Vettii in Pompeii. The background painting depicts the two *lares* with a cornucopia and a drinking bowl, between them the *Genius* of the head of the household, and a snake.

One peculiarity of the *lares* was their accessibility: in conservative Roman households, only the head of the household and his family could sacrifice to the gods. But the *lares* were also responsible for the rest of the household who were permitted to worship them and make sacrifices. Hence images of the *lares* were often found in the kitchens of larger households, and in the living quarters of servants and slaves. These unprivileged groups primarily celebrated the feast of *Compitalia*, named after the Latin word for crossroads. During these winter festivities, the *lares* of each crossroads as well as the surrounding property, houses, and farmland were all honoured. The crossroads were often the site of small altars, like today's wayside shrines.

The entire household, including its head, would make sacrifices to the *lares* in their role as household spirits. The records document a wide range of occasions for these sacrifices, and the potential offerings: they include the sacrifice of a protective amulet, the *bulla*, which Roman boys wore until they reached manhood; girls ritually sacrificing their dolls for the same reason; and the offering of a copper coin by a newly wedded wife on entering the house for the first time after her marriage. In earlier periods, daily sacrifices of incense, bread, porridge, milk, and wine are also documented. According to an old popular belief, food that fell from the table had to be sacrificed to the *lares* to avert misfortune befalling the household.

The *lares* themselves are depicted as youths, sometimes children wearing *bulla*, the special amulet for boys. They almost always carry a cornucopia from which they are filling a drinking bowl and are usually dancing. The Roman literature described these protective spirits as joyful, laughing and dancing. This depiction of laughing and dancing children was true for both the family *lares* as well as the protectors of fields, crossroads, plots of land, and communities. The *lares* were also often portrayed either with, or as, snakes.

The *lares* were accompanied by the *penates*, the protective spirits of the household stores. In modern literature the *penates* are always named in conjunction with the *lares*, although their role as protective beings was far less extensive, with references to them in the contemporary sources correspondingly rare. They are particularly known from the myth of the founding of Rome, when Aeneas, ancestor of Romulus and Remus, the city's founders, brought the *penates* from Troy to Italy.

Over time the *penates* developed into guardians of food, drink, and the hearth, the latter together with the *lares* and the *vesta*. Which of these spirits was actually worshipped in any given household probably depended upon the specific time, place, and family tradition.

The counterparts to these helpful and protective beings were the *larvae* and *lemures*. The meaning of these words was originally disputed, even by the Roman authors themselves, but from the time of Augustus they had become evil spirits which, depending on the explanation, emerged from the bodies of the dead. These beings could frighten and pester humans almost anywhere, but their scene of action was primarily the underworld. As a result of attempts to systematize the terminology, the originally separate terms became linked and partly combined: the *lares* as good, protective spirits; the *larvae* as evil spirits; and the *lemures* as *Genii* turned into *larvae*. To this are added the *manes*, generally understood to be the spirits of the dead. Authors through the ages have used all these terms synonymously which introduces contamination to the mythology. This form of contamination is highly reminiscent of the diversity of other legendary figures, including the German household spirits.

Following the introduction of the *Codex Theodosianus* in 312 AD, the worship of all pagan deities and idols was officially forbidden. By the end of the fourth century, at a time in which the worship of the old gods had already faded into the past, and with their demise finally sealed by this imperial law, Church Father Hieronymus still complained that the rural population sacrificed to idols in their houses, *"quos domesticos apellant lares"* / "which the household inhabitants called *lares*" (Hier., In Iasiam, LVII, VII). Even though the tradition of individual spirits of the house was ignored in favor of Christian tradition in the following centuries, this last flash of the *lares* in a Christianized time is nevertheless an indication of a possible, unbroken tradition of the house spirits up to antiquity.

Tobias Janouschek M.A.
Archaeo GmbH
Randenstraße 12
78234 Engen-Welschingen

Textual and Archaeological Evidence for Belief in Household Spirits in the Medieval Period

Professor Tobias Gärtner

Even in antiquity, supernatural beings were believed to reside in human houses. The Romans called them *penates*. They also honoured house gods, or *lares*, the *Genius* of the head of the household and the ancestors, all of whom watched over the wellbeing of the household (see contribution by Tobias Janouschek). The sacrificial acts can sometimes be proven archaeologically, for example when, as is the case with rare finds from Switzerland, a ceramic mug was buried under the fireplace together with a coin. As these objects were no longer accessible once the hearth had been constructed, they cannot be mistaken for storage vessels or hiding places. Instead, they are more likely to indicate a building sacrifice. These sacrifices also took other forms, such as offerings buried in a wall, under the foundation of a wall, or under a threshold, so that the gods would protect the house and its occupants. Archaeologists are familiar with this sort of religious practice, not only within the Roman Empire, but also from the Germanic peoples beyond the boundaries of the empire. Although textual sources say nothing on the subject, there is archaeological evidence which can be directly linked to the house and building sacrifices of the Roman world. Under a hearth in Dorsten-Holsterhausen (district of Recklinghausen), for example, a vessel was discovered that had clearly contained a sacrificial offering (no longer preserved). The placing of objects in the area around the hearth was also found during the Migration Period between 375 and 568 AD. A house in Tinnum, on the island of Sylt, had a fireplace paved with stones. A large pot was buried under the stones, and beside it a flint knife. This could indicate a ritual practice, as both items were inaccessible after the hearth was built.

With the advent of the Christian religion, there was no longer any place in everyday life for honouring the old Roman and Germanic household deities and spirits. Grace was still said before meals, but no share of the food was sacrificed to God. Even so, the old notions of household spirits with the power to influence inhabitants' lives in a variety of ways remained active amongst parts of the population, although this can only be established from textual sources for the Central European region from around 1000 AD.

Rather than inexplicably resurging after an interruption of several centuries in what were then Christianized regions, it is more probable that the belief in household

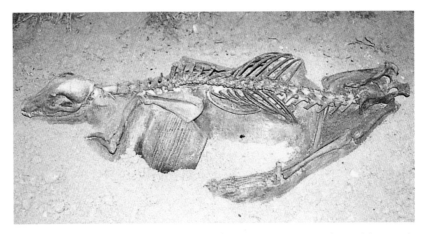

Building sacrifice of dog and ceramic pot, circa 1300 (Leipzig, Preussergässchen: Fehring, 1996).

spirits persisted through the early medieval period. It must be assumed that the belief in spirits continued, although the actual content of these beliefs may well have changed substantially. The chronicler Thietmar von Merseburg (975 – 1018) reports of the region around Fallersleben: "For the inhabitants there, who seldom go to church, pay little heed to visits from their clergy. They honour house deities (*domesticos deos*) and sacrifice to them in the hope of their assistance." Clearly, the people saw in these beings not (only) the malevolent demons, as would have corresponded to Christian teaching, but also helpful spirits.

Between 1236 and 1250, the Silesian Cistercian monk Rudolph wrote: "When moving into new houses they bury pots in the earth, in various corners and sometimes behind the hearth, filled with different things for the household spirits, who the people call Stetewaldiu (ruler of the place), and they do not allow anything to be poured behind the hearth. And sometimes they throw some of their food there so that they reconcile with the inhabitants of the house. Should we not call this idolatry?" This is a key text for understanding the archaeological finds which we can associate with a belief in household spirits.

Michael Beheim wrote the following verse circa 1460: "Many also believe / their house contains a schretlein / who looks after / those who treat it well." A household spirit might be helpful, but by the same token, it could also be evil. While we can distinguish two separate origins for these beliefs, they can rarely be unambiguously identified in the sources: the household spirit is either the soul of a dead ancestor, or a spirit that is guarding a specific place. After a house was built at that place, an offering would be made to the spirit to propitiate it.

Although the textual sources offer us good arguments to read the archaeological finds, their interpretation is often anything but simple and unequivocal. A key question always remains about whether other magical practices, not related to a belief in household spirits, were the reason for depositing the discovered objects.

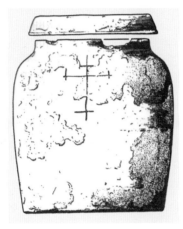

Saulgau, Schützenstrasse 7, ceramic pot with incised cross potent from a cellar wall
(after Scholkmann 1981).

For example, a vessel buried in front of a door may relate to a magic curse. In 1516 such a case was reported in Hannover. On trial for witchcraft, Geseke Stolle admitted that she "had buried a pot in front of the doorstep belonging to Arnd Krudener's wife, together with an old dagger that had magic in it, and five weeks before Shrove Tuesday had dug it up again, as advised by her confessor."

Despite uncertainties about the precise details, the archaeological finds clearly show that during the medieval period practices were carried out which were clearly a continuation of ancient ritual sacrifices. Likewise, there are always fireplaces dating to the medieval period under which pots are buried in such a manner that can

only be interpreted as a ritual deposit. In a thirteenth-century farmhouse in Ickern (district of Castrop-Rauxel), a hearth measuring 60 x 60 cm at ground level was paved with stones. Under a lateral cavity in the paving were found three pots buried next to one another, and with the mouths of the vessels facing downwards. It is not certain whether the clay covering the paving also concealed the area with the pots, but in any case, the interior of the pots was not accessible after construction of the hearth. In Lübeck, at Fischstrasse 10, the crushed remains of a vessel dating from the second half of the twelfth century were found under a layer of clay over a hearth. Similarly, at Burgstrasse 16 in Hannover, an upright pot dating from the late thirteenth/early fourteenth century, covered by a large shard of pottery was discovered under a hearth. A few centimetres to the side of the hearth, a small jug was hidden under the floor.

There are also countless finds of so-called ash vessels, buried at ground level alongside hearths, into which the ashes from the fire could be tipped. Lying with their openings at floor height, they were clearly regularly emptied, and therefore accessible which proves that these are different from sacrificial vessels. During the excavation of the small jug in Hannover, it was not recorded whether the top of the jug was on level with the floor, or beneath it. However, as the vessel was very small and had a narrow neck, it would appear unsuitable for collecting ashes, and so we must assume we are looking at the remains of a hearth sacrifice.

There is also archaeological evidence of building sacrifices placed in other parts of the house. These often took the form of vessels buried below the foundations and could therefore only have been placed there during the construction of the house (Göttingen, Lüneburg, Templin). For instance, at Grapengiesserstrasse 41 in Lüneburg, a globular pot dating to the thirteenth century was found "in the area of the foundations." It contained a Stone Age ceramic flask. We cannot say with any certainty how this was related to the house builder's beliefs: the flask may have been discovered in a Stone Age megalithic tomb—was this seen as an object of pagan ancestry, whose spirits now had to be appeased? Findings from Saulgau, in the district of Sigmaringen, indicate that people also saw a need to defend themselves against household spirits. There, in the fifteenth century, an unusually shaped lidded vessel was found embedded in a cellar wall and appears to have been built specifically for that purpose. A cross was engraved on its exterior, suggesting a defence against evil spirits. Clearly, the intention was to confine a spirit of the place to the interior of the vessel.

Most of these finds are linked to a belief in spirits of a place and household spirits, yet there are a much larger number of deposits which could equally well be related to other magical beliefs. Where pots or large jugs are found buried upright in the ground, and with no other specific characteristics, these may well relate to placenta burials. The custom of burying the placenta in the cellar of the house or other places in order to protect the mother and child from harm continued into the early twentieth century. We already know of such deposits from the medieval period (Cloister of the Augustine Hermits at Neustadt an der Orla), supported by scientific analysis. Consequently, the reasons behind hiding or burying vessels about the house are often unclear: the Altmarkt in Dresden and the Buttergasse in Magdeburg are such examples, dating from the High and Late Medieval Periods.

In 1271, a wooden castle tower was built in Eschelbronn, near Heidelberg, with the site first being sealed with a layer of clay. The skull of a horse was buried in this layer. It was clearly already skeletal when placed there, for the lower jawbone had been removed, turned, and laid under the upper jaw. After the tower was built, the skull was no longer accessible, which at first suggests that it was a building sacrifice to propitiate the spirit of the place. However, now we know from modern sources that horse skulls were believed to serve as defences against diseases and lighting strikes. If that was the case in Eschelbronn, then the deposit is not related to any belief in spirits.

Deposits of animals or parts of their bodies inside or around a house are more frequent occurrences. During an excavation in Nabburg (Oberpfalz), a dog was found buried in an exterior cellar wall dating back to the late medieval period. It was laid on its back and decapitated prior to burial. Its body had been weighted down with small stones. This is reminiscent of special human burials in which large stones were laid on the corpse, a practice associated with fear of the person rising from the dead. Could there have been a similar anxiety that this dog would return? While the archaeologist who discovered this dog believed it was a building sacrifice, it is not at all clear that this is the case. Although animal skeletons are frequently found buried under floors within houses, they should not be immediately interpreted as building sacrifices.

Instead, it is about the usual domestic animals (cow, pig, horse) which deceased or did not appear fit for human consumption and so have been hastily buried in the yard. As residential areas became more densely built, newer buildings were constructed on such areas, so that today the bodies are found under the floor of later houses, tempting us to assume that animal sacrifices had also been offered here. We are often presented with finds whose significance is difficult to determine.

This paper can only provide a brief insight into the archaeological evidence which offers us some idea of the nature of the belief in household spirits in Germany in the medieval period. It is clear how difficult it can be to interpret the finds in specific cases. Despite this, the study of archaeological and textual sources clearly shows that people believed in household spirits and offered sacrifices to them in the medieval period, while sometimes also seeing in them evil demons needing to be banished. In the medieval period, as in modern times, a multiplicity of magical practices existed alongside a belief in spirits, which likewise have left their traces in the ground.

Tobias Gärtner
Professor of Medieval and Modern Archaeology
Martin Luther University in Halle-Wittenberg
Emil Abderhalden Strasse 26/27
06108 Halle (Saale)

Large Trolls, Small Trolls, Household Spirits

Professor Rudolf Simek

In medieval Scandinavia, trolls are large, dangerous creatures which are almost exclusively harmful to humans. They steal food, abduct women, and are deadly opponents in battle, even for heroes. In the Viking period, anyone saying "May the trolls take you!" was uttering a very serious death wish, one even more powerful than expression: "May the Devil take you!" Troll lifestyles differ completely from those of humans: they may celebrate their festivals, and sometimes actually have children (mostly evil and magically large) or act as foster mothers, but they are certainly not very social.

As the medieval period progressed, however, trolls began to change, even appearing as attractive, and often helpful, females in the Icelandic sagas. In the sixteenth century, Olaf Magnus, in his monumental *Historia de gentibus septentrionalibus* ("Description of the Northern Peoples"), describes trolls as large, or conversely small beings, who live underground. Presaging the two main directions in which these beliefs would develop in Scandinavia in modern times, Magnus portrays the trolls as large where he identifies them as having been turned into stone in mountain cliffs or on the Swedish coast. But when he places them in mines and caves, he describes them as small, as demons living under the earth, and he even conflates them with dwarfs and elves.

A miner can be seen working on the left side of the picture, whereas a troll is visible on the right.

In the modern era, these two very different versions of trolls in Scandinavian folk beliefs resulted in the appearance of gigantic trolls in Swedish and Danish folktales. Although, like the trolls of Norwegian folktales, they are huge creatures, tall as trees, they are stupid, and they can be vanquished by crafty heroes. In the sagas, these trolls are responsible for building huge, prehistoric structures, or for placing the inexplicable boulders found lying around the countryside. In Sweden they were sometimes simply described as living in the forest. In Denmark, at the same time, whole family clans of small trolls appear in the early modern age who reportedly lived in grave mounds where at night they could sometimes be heard holding huge celebrations together.

Trolls as household spirits and spirits of the earth.

The small trolls of the Danish legends and folktales are most akin to the continental European concept of *wichtel* and *heinzelmännchen*, although they also merge with other Scandinavian beings (though only in the modern age) such as *hulders* or *nisse*. Although they spend most of the lives apart from humans, living in prehistoric grave mounds widespread in the Danish landscape, these small trolls play a role as household spirits.

These little trolls, collectively known as *Trold*, as well as *Bjærgfolk* or *Ellefolk*, "mount -ain people" or "elven people" in Danish, live in human-like social structures. They have families and children, and are engaged in typical rural occupations, although as artisans rather than farmers. This is a characteristic they share with dwarfs, and this is also the reason why sometimes the sound of pounding, like that in a black-smith's workshop, is heard emanating from the hills. These shy creatures are extraor-dinarily helpful to humans: female trolls help human women during difficult births, and sometimes assist older people with tasks that demand strength, such as harvesting hay or repairing agricultural machinery.

Theodor Severin Kittelsen, *Troll wonders how old he is*,
Neo-Romantic mythological painting, 1911.

Occasionally, they need help from humans and can demonstrate extreme gratitude for that assistance. Just like the heinzelmännchen, when treated properly they look after the wellbeing of the household. Now and again, they display kobold-like traits, with folktales accusing them of being responsible for the overnight disappearance of tools or food. And, if badly treated, angered, or spied on, they can become aggressive and malicious: farmhouses built with stones taken from the trolls' (grave) mounds are burned to the ground, or haunted by the now-homeless small trolls. Life is made so unpleasant for the humans that they might be driven away.

In contrast to the large trolls, which Scandinavian folktales and sagas describe as large and sometimes having several heads, the most characteristic feature of small Danish trolls is not just their limited size, but also one of their garments, namely the red cap which they clearly share with today's garden gnomes. In Scandinavia, by the Late Medieval Period at the latest, it is certain that the term "troll" became an overall term describing all possible types of otherworldly beings in folklore, from the huge evil trolls of the Icelandic sagas and Norwegian fairy tales to the small household spirits with their red caps in modern Danish folktales.

Prof. Dr. Rudolf Simek
University of Bonn
Institute for German Studies
Department of Scandinavian studies
Am Hof 1d
D - 53113 Bonn

Die Irischen Elfenmärchen of the Brothers Grimm

Burkhard Kling

Jacob and Wilhelm Grimm are famous for their collection of *Children's and Household Tales*, first published in 1812. The book was certainly not intended as a collection of bedtime stories for children, as it is often seen today. The first edition contained eighty-five fairy tales, with fifty-eight pages of annotations. It was a scientific book, designed for libraries and linguistic researchers. A second volume was issued in 1815. There were seven editions in total during the Brothers Grimm's lifetime, with Wilhelm Grimm himself editing the seventh and last edition which appeared in 1857.

Nowadays, the children's fairy tales and folklore written by the Brothers Grimm are amongst the most frequently printed books in German. The collection contains many stories about household spirits and elf-like beings—here are just a few examples: "The Three Dwarfs" (KHM 13), "The Elves and the Shoemaker" (KHM 39), "Snow White" (KHM 53), and "Rumpelstiltskin" (KHM 55).

The lesser-known collection of fairy tales by the Brothers Grimm, published in 1826: *Die Irischen Elfenmärchen* ("Tales of Irish Elves") was issued by the Friedrich Fleischer publishing house in Leipzig. In it, the Brothers Grimm referred to themselves as merely the translators of the work, it being based on the Fairy Legends and Traditions of South Ireland by Thomas Crofton Croker (1798 – 1854). Croker was an Irish antiquarian who collected old poems, songs, and folklore from Irish culture, and supported the founding of literary and language societies. He and his wife investigated burial and funeral rituals.

The extensive introduction to *Die Irischen Elfenmärchen*, dated 1825, appeared in the same year as the English original. Croker published two further volumes of his collection of texts in 1828, although these were not of interest to the Grimm brothers or translated into German. Interestingly, in his third volume, Croker published an English translation of the introduction which the Grimm brothers wrote for their Irish fairy tales, as well as further commentary from his correspondence with Wilhelm Grimm.

The Grimm brothers prefixed the Irish fairy tales with an extensive introduction. According to their own statements, the Grimms shortened everything in Croker's editorial notes which did not relate to the tales they were translating, instead beginning their introduction with a description of the various Irish beliefs in elves, according to which the tales then follow.

This is followed by a longer discourse on William Grant Stewart's (1797 – 1869) "*The popular superstitions and festive amusements of the Highlanders of Scotland*" (Edinburgh: 1823), and other sources. The preface and introduction are often missing in current editions of *Die Irischen Elfenmärchen*; apparently, this lengthy portrayal of the lives and environment of elves is no longer topical.

The preface is written like a serious paper about elves and begins as follows:

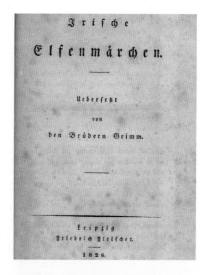

Die Irischen Elfenmärchen by the Brothers Grimm was published in 1826.

"The elves, who in their true form are scarcely one-inch tall, have airy, almost transparent bodies, so delicate that when the elves jump onto a drop of dew it certainly trembles, but does not flow away. Both male and female elves are extremely beautiful, beyond comparison with mortal humans. They do not live alone or in pairs, but always in large social groups. They are invisible to humans, especially in daytime, and so can be present, listening to what people say. Therefore, they should only be mentioned carefully and with respect, and addressed only as good folk or friends, for any other name would offend them."

Preface
Introduction—About the Elves
Elves in Ireland

1. The Good People
2. The Cluricaun
3. The Banshee
4. The Phuka
5. The Country of the Young

Elves in Scotland

1. Origins
2. Form
3. Home and Way of Life
4. Relationship with Humans
5. Craftsmanship
6. Good Neighbours
7. Malicious Tricks
8. Changelings
9. Elf Arrow, Weapons, and Tools
10. The Elf Animal
11. Sea Elves
12. The Brownie

On the Nature of Elves

I. Name
II. Gradation and Diversity
III. Demise
IV. Form
V. Clothing
VI. Home
VII. Language
VIII. Food
IX. Way of Life
X. Secret Powers and Craftsmanship
XI. Character
XII. Relationship with Humans
XIII. Hostile Attitude
XIV. Old Evidence
XV. Elfin Animals
XVI. Witches and Fiends

After the preface and detailed analysis of the variety of elf types in the introduction, twenty-seven tales were presented under the following groupings: *The Good People* (eleven tales), *The Cluricaun* (five tales), *The Banshee* (two tales), *The Phuka* (four tales), and *The Country of the Young* (five tales). Each tale is followed by additional commentary.

Although in their classification the Brothers Grimm clearly separated and discussed the Irish and Scottish traditions, it is the Irish tales that are printed in this edition. As well as the chapters on *The Good People* and *The Country of the Young*, the tales focus on three types of elves: the *cluricaun*, the *banshee*, and the *phuka*.

A *cluricaun* is an elfin being from Ireland's Celtic mythology. It is closely related to the leprechaun, a kobold, which, as a spirit of the natural world, is often associated with hidden gold at the end of the rainbow and is an emblem of Ireland. Thomas Crofton Croker derived the name from the word *luchramán*, for dwarf. Today *cluricaun* is a common name for an Irish pub.

The word "*banshee*" derived from Irish-Gaelic and means something like "woman from the hills," which is actually synonymous for a fairy figure. In Celtic mythology and Irish folklore, the *banshee* is a female spirit whose appearance heralds impending death. In Scotland, the banshee washes the bloodied clothes or armour of the dying fighter, thus foretelling their imminent death. She appears alone, and is deadly pale and dressed in white, often portrayed as an old woman with long hair, either black or white. Her eyes are often bloodshot from constant weeping. She is more often heard than seen and mostly sits weeping in front of a family's window a few days before the death of a family member. Often her screeching can drive listeners mad. The person whose death the *banshee* foretells does not hear her lament. Instead, the *banshee* is gentle and comforting to the soul whom she will soon welcome into the realm of the dead.

The *phuka* are also creatures from Celtic mythology. They are relatively harmless spirits or kobolds, mischievous and skilled in wizardry, who live underground together with gnomes and dwarfs. In Ireland, *phuka* appear to humans particularly at Samhain, one of the four great Gaelic festivals, celebrated on November first, but with celebrations beginning on the evening of October thirty-first. *Phuka* are shapeshifters, every now and then appearing to humans in the form of different animals, perhaps a dog, goat, or horse, but always with dark coats. Their favourite manifestation is as a black pony. *Phuka* invite unwary travellers for a ride which quickly turns into a totally terrifying cross-country journey for the unsuspecting traveller, over hill and dale, and through thorny undergrowth. Most *phuka* throw their victims off somewhere on the moor and disappear amid peals of laughter. However, sometimes they also warn of disaster.

The Brothers Grimm also studied spirit beings other than those in Irish folktales. Jacob Grimm's *Deutsche Mythologie* first appeared in 1835; this important and trailblazing work continues to guide and lay the foundations for linguistic scholars and cultural historians studying religious history and mythology. In chapter XVII of this book, Jacob Grimm dedicates almost thirty pages to gnomes and elves, describing their history and literary references.

Much of what we know about spirits, elves, dwarfs, and kobolds we have learned from the Brothers Grimm, through their fairy tales, as well as their scientific studies, and careful analysis of historical texts. Without them and their works, our imaginations, fantasies, and mythical world would be significantly poorer.

Burkhard Kling
Art Historian
Director of the Brüder Grimm-Haus Museum Steinau
Brüder-Grimm-Strasse 80
36396 Steinau an der Strasse
Germany

The Changeling—A Fiend in the Cradle

Janin Pisarek

"Sometimes demonic powers steal a human child and put another in its place."

From Piaschewski, Gisela (1938): *Art. Wechselbalg. In: Handwörterbuch des Deutschen Aberglaubens.* Vol. 9. Berlin 1938, p. 835–864.

A REPLACED CHILD

The term "changeling" refers to a creature left behind by some demonic being after the theft of a human newborn. Although the changeling looks like a child, it may be very old. In German folklore, this exchange usually takes place during the first six weeks of an infant's life. The concept of changelings endured over centuries. It is particularly a motif found in legends and folktales, but also appearing in fairy tales and ballads, predominantly in Northern and Central Europe, and the Slavic regions. It is likely that tales of changelings outside these regions are the result of European influence.

"Every malformed child was generally regarded to be a changeling, and in the six-teenth and seventeenth centuries even highly educated people were convinced of their existence."

From F. A. Brockhaus (1841). *Brockhaus Bilder-Conversations-Lexikon.* Vol. 4. Leipzig, p. 675.

In popular belief recorded well into the nineteenth century, the changeling is an ugly creature with a malformed body; pale, aged face; large eyes; and thick, wide lips. It was said that it seldom lived long, and hardly grew. Sometimes it is insatiable, learns slowly and walks awkwardly. It seems developmentally disabled, screaming or muttering incomprehensible words.

The Changeling

A child with a large head the size of a pumpkin,
Light blond moustache, aged pigtail,
With long, spidery, but strong little arms,
A huge stomach, though short bowels,
A changeling, that a corporal
Secretly laid in our cradle—
In place of the baby whom he stole,
The deformed creature, who with the falsehood,

With his beloved windchimes perhaps,
Fathered by the old sodomite—
I do not need to name the monstrosity—
You should drown or burn it!

Heinrich Heine, *Werke und Briefe in zehn Bänden.* Vol. 1, (Berlin and Weimar: 1972) p. 332–333.

According to tradition, it was mostly elfish creatures who exchanged a human baby for a changeling. The exchange was performed by a wide variety of spirits, including household spirits. Forest and water spirits, and phantom apparitions were also said to hunger for human offspring. The Church usually demonized these beings, as is frequently seen in Luther's writings:

"Satan lays changelings in the place of proper children to torment the people. He often drags scores of young maids into the water, makes them pregnant, and keeps them with him until they give birth, then placing these same children in the cradle and taking away the real children. But it is said that such changelings do not live more than eighteen or nineteen years."

From Luther's *Table Talk*, 20.4.1539

EXCHANGE AND EXPULSION

A variety of actions and objects promised protection against the abduction of infants. As well as baptism and blessing the mother, they included burning candles, iron and silver objects, a crucifix, or the Bible. The list of protective objects is almost endless, although in some stories the spirits succeed in their quest to steal a child through some form of subterfuge.

"According to popular belief, children must be watched over carefully before they are baptized, because otherwise they could be exchanged. Every newborn child must sneeze, but if the parents fail to immediately say 'God help me,' the Devil comes and exchanges the child with a changeling."

From Karl Friedrich Wilhelm Wander (1876): *Deutsches Sprichwörter-Lexikon.* Vol. 4. Leipzig, p. 1840.

If the child was taken and replaced by a changeling, it was usually only invocations and magic that could help recover the stolen infant. Along with Christian signs, two other possibilities are specified for exposing the changeling and getting rid of it. One involves violence, where the changeling is beaten with nine hazel rods until it bleeds, is swept out of the house or thrown into water or fire, all to force the return of the baby. The violence against the changeling causes the spirit to return the infant.

The second, more usual way was to trick the changeling into speaking or laughing by performing a strange and absurd action. For example, sweeping with the handle of a broom, cooking odd ingredients such as shoe soles, or brewing beer in eggshells. These would make the changeling speak or laugh, betraying its name or age. In a legend from Lower Saxony recorded by folklorists Georg Schambach (1811 – 1879) and Wilhelm Konrad Hermann Müller (1812 – 1890), the changeling shouts: "I'm as old as the Thuringian forest, and never in all my life have I seen a woman brew beer in eggshells!"

A mother discovers the changeling. "The Changeling" by Henry Fuseli (1780), Kunsthaus Zürich.

LIVING BELIEF AND LIVED PRACTISE

"The superstition associated with exchanged children illustrates the search for an explanation for an abnormal human appearance using the means available to the primitive spirit: its source is fear."

From Piaschewski, Gisela (1938): *Art. Wechselbalg.* In: HdA. Vol. 9, p. 860f.

Sudden pathological changes in a baby's appearance have probably always aroused the human need for an explanation. Simple thought processes turn one object into two—the concept of a healthy child and a diseased child. The tales dramatically condense the comparatively short time in which these significant differences present themselves, finally taking the form of an exchange. Medieval treatises support this thought process, linking the idea of a changeling to the concepts of incubus and succubus magic. Gisela Piaschewski, whose 1935 dissertation provided the most comprehensive work in the German language on changelings at that time noted that in the German-speaking area in the eleventh century, the "superstitious notion of changeling—also in a magical sense" (Piaschewski 1938, p. 864) was an accepted tradition.

Striving to purify the Christian world, Luther advised the Prince of Anhalt to drown changelings. Many other clergy, considering the changeling to be a real phenomenon and treating it as a theological issue, advised that deformed children should be thrown on the rubbish heap, into the stove, or into the water. These practices reached their zenith in the period from the fifteenth to the seventeenth centuries, coinciding with the persecution of witches. These beliefs lingered on up to the nineteenth century, resulting in handicapped or deformed children being mistreated or killed.

In 1898, the Austrian criminologist and criminal lawyer, Hans Gustav Adolf Gross (1847 – 1915) reported:

"Belief in the changeling (Kielkopf) is remarkably enduring [. . .] The evil in this practice is that it is paired with the conviction that the changeling must be beaten or tormented until the one who brought the changeling comes back to collect it, returning the stolen child. Wuttke, Schwarz, Mannhardt, Löwenstimm, and many other writers have recorded such enough of these cases that Russian legislators found it necessary to explicitly forbid the killing of deformed children in Article 1469 of the Russian criminal code. I once had the opportunity of experiencing just how popular the belief in changelings remains."

From Gross, Hans (1898): *Aberglaube und Verbrechen. In: Die Gartenlaube, Illustriertes Familienblatt.* No. 38. p. 505–508, p. 506f.

The Devil steals a child and replaces it with a changeling. Excerpt from *The Legend of St. Stephen*, painting by Martino di Bartolomeo (early fifteenth century).

Gross explains that in his jurisdiction a woman had been brought to court charged with negligent homicide, having hanged her tightly bound child in the cradle. She was reported to have calmly stated that she was completely innocent, because "the Devil did it." He had tried to exchange her newborn for a changeling but, having got it tangled up in the cords, fled. Several neighbours confirmed the truth of this statement.

Children accused of being changelings were often suffering from endemic diseases caused by underactive thyroid function. This included goitre, an abnormality usually described as "cretinism," which causes the patient to die young—or for which it is killed. The physician Johannes Hartlieb (around 1400 – 1468) made the first attempts to view the changeling as a sick child, rather than a demonic being, referring to the disease as *bolismus* or *apetitus caninus.* However, such explanations had little impact. It was only when the surgeon and anatomist Lorenz Heister (1683 – 1758)

explained that changelings were children with rickets that the concept of illness gained traction, even though the physical changes were largely the consequence of other diseases.

From 1851 onwards, the polymath and physician Rudolf Virchow (1821 – 1902) examined cretinism based on surveys from Lower Franconia from the year 1840. The total number of cases reported at that time was 133, or one in 4,355 inhabitants. Virchow's investigations confirmed that the locals lied about the existence of cretins, and thus he suspected that the actual number of those affected was considerably higher. He described the eighteen-year-old Wilhelm Scheid in Wiesenbronn as the most "horrific" cretin he saw in Franconia:

"He sat huddled on a windowsill, his head sunk on his chest [. . .] over a pot placed under him as he constantly soiled himself. His outward appearance was that of a monstrous child, for his whole length was short of two-and-a-half shoes [approx. seventy-three cm] and his head, covered with sparse, light, short, dry, dull hair, suggested at first glance the condition of a youth. We had difficulty raising his head and then saw his ugly [. . .] face."

From Virchow, Rudolf (2007): *Sämtliche Werke, Eds. Christian Andree, Abt. I.* Vol. 16.2. Hildesheim, p. 891–969.

The record from 1840 shows that even during this period two doctors were of the view that demonic influences were involved in cretinism. As in the traditional legends and popular beliefs about changelings, such children were often severely neglected and at times cruelly treated in the hope that the biological mother of the supernatural child would bring back the human child in exchange for her own.

It would be several decades more before thyroid extracts could be successfully applied to treat goitres and cretinism, and the search for the active component in the thyroid began. Thyroxin was synthesized for the first time in 1926, enabling the iodine deficiency which caused the underactive thyroid function to be prevented, and its dreadful consequences, both physical and social, to be averted.

CONCLUSION

Are the reports of changelings true? We do not know, but many storytellers obviously had plenty of material on the subject. It was clear how attempts to explain unknown illnesses became rooted in popular belief, and how these beliefs were expressed in practice. This is where the fear of the "strange" and "other" played a major role—in legends from the medieval period through to the nineteenth century,

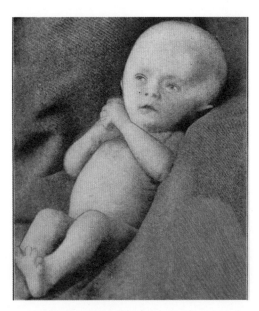

Child with genetic hydrocephalus (also called water on the brain, or dropsy). Photographed in Sheffield, Herman Bernard (1871): Modern diagnosis and treatment of diseases of children; a treatise on the medical and surgical diseases of infancy and childhood.

disturbing behaviour and abnormal appearances were linked to the motif of newborn exchanges carried out by numinous figures. The perspective of the changelings themselves, and the reason they sought attention in the form of overeating and screaming, is completely missing from the logic of the legends.

Sermons had far-reaching effects on popular belief, lending the phenomenon of the changeling not only a reality, but also giving it a historical tradition, one which reached its zenith during witch trials. The trial records show how the subject matter of oral traditions infiltrated people's everyday lives. The example of the changeling also shows the difficulty of creating acceptance of medical knowledge and upper-case enlightenment trends in the face of strongly held religious views and firmly anchored popular beliefs. This challenge can be traced right up until the nineteenth, and even into the twentieth century.

Janin Pisarek, M.A.
Narrative Researcher
Project & Cultural Mananger at
Landesvereinigung Kulturelle Jugendbildung Thüringen

Spooks and Ghostly Apparitions of the Past and Present

Eberhard Bauer

"The pack of devils by no rules is daunted:
We are so wise, and yet is Tegel haunted."
Goethe: *Faust I (Walpurgis Night)*, Verse 4160f.

Reports of ghosts, apparitions, and phantoms date back to ancient times and can be observed in many cultures. For centuries, interpretations of these phenomena have mirrored the dominant social, religious, and cultural ideologies, and collective attitudes. Detailed descriptions of phenomena that, according to the typical reports and events, we would today call spectres or poltergeists date back to seventeenth and eighteenth–century Europe, particularly in England, France, and Germany. They were (and are) the subject of studies of reception or mentality, particularly from a historical, religious, or literary perspective. Reports of spectres and ghostly apparitions have a special place in discourses on the social role of superstition (*superstitio*) in the historical context of magic, demonology, and witchcraft in the early modern age, and in the looming conflicts with the rationality ushered in during the Enlightenment. It is in this area of conflict in which early and sometimes detailed reports of apparitions are presented in compendiums on the topic (cf. Gauld & Cornell, 2017). One example from this era is the famous Drummer of Tedworth, a ghostly apparition dating from 1662 – 1663, which the Anglican priest and philosopher Joseph Glanvil wrote about in *Sadducismus Triumphatus* (1681), his influential volume on demonology. Florian Bertram Gerstmann (cf. Puhle, 1998/1999, p. 24–26) provides us with a comprehensive, 159-page report of a ghostly "rain of stones" in Dortmund, falling in the house of a Lutheran physician over a period of several weeks in 1713.

The Swabian physician and poet Justinus Kerner (1786 – 1862) is a pioneer of "early" nineteenth-century research into ghostly apparitions; in his 1836 publication *Eine Erscheinung aus dem Nachtgebiete der Natur* he provides a detailed description of ghostly activities occurring between 1835 and 1836 in the former county court of Weinsberg, affecting a thirty-nine-year-old female prisoner. Kerner's detailed description of the phenomenon includes a whole range of typical ghostly noises, including steps, rustling, dripping, loud bangs, the throwing of sand, beating wings, shaking, and clanking, as well as a noise reminiscent of "beams falling from a cellar ceiling." Kerner was careful to separate "natural facts" from fraud, illusions, or

"psychological contamination" as well as interpreting such phenomena in terms of "ghostly suppositions" (cf. Bauer, 1989). Another equally prominent apparition in the history of famous nineteenth century ghosts was that experienced by advocate and member of the National Assembly, Melchior Joller, in Stans, Lake Lucerne, in 1862, and recorded by Fanny Moser (1977, p. 43–148).

Joller described in detail the mystical appearances he experienced in his 1863 *Darstellung selbsterlebter mystischer Erscheinungen*. This was used as the basis for the 2003 televised mystery documentary *Das Spukhaus* (Volker Anding).

Illustration of apparitions in Cideville, France, 1850 – 1851. Illustration from Damien, Michel (Ed.) (1978): *Les hôtes invisibles: les dossiers noirs des maisons hantées*. Tchou, Paris, p. 22

The collection and examination of ghostly apparitions is also a task for the Society for Psychical Research (SPR), founded in London in 1882 and still active. Its members were famous scholars of their time, although the opinions of the SPR researchers did vary. Based on his own experience, the physicist Sir William Barrett claimed such appearances were real, while Frank Podmore declared that well-documented cases in SPR material were fraudulent deceptions—the kobold-like and mischievous nature of these phenomena, with their partly infantile aggression, were more reminiscent of tricks played by a "naughty little girl," his favoured hypothesis. The same dichotomy of opinions continues into the present day, as the controversial assessment of the "Enfield Poltergeist" which captivated British audiences from 1977 – 1978 impressively demonstrates (cf. Willin, 2019).

Over its history, the Freiburger Institute for Frontier Areas of Psychology and Mental Health (IGPP), founded by psychology professor Hans Bender (1907 – 1991) in 1950, has examined numerous apparitions and helped thousands of people who, unsettled by apparently inexplicable events, have turned to the institute for information and advice. In a popular survey conducted on behalf of the IGPP asking more than 1,500 adult Germans about personal experiences of extraordinary events, twelve percent answered "yes" when asked if they had ever experienced things behaving oddly in their presence, or other strange things which had given them the feeling that a place was haunted.

Poltergeist in the shape of kobold-like beings. Illustration by Hookham, Frontispiece in Price, Harry (1945) Poltergeist over England.

There are many reports of things behaving "oddly" in everyday life. In the hierarchy of strangeness, they include the following cases (quoted according to Bender, 1970):

(1) Bombardment: often a house becomes the target of a hail of shots. Stones fall on the roof, break windows, and enter the house through openings.
(2) Knocking noises, banging against doors, walls, or furniture can be heard, sometimes localized, sometimes all over the house.
(3) Doors, windows, and even carefully closed cupboards open themselves.
(4) Objects are carefully moved or tipped over, delicate objects often remain unharmed, even after a jump of several metres, while solid objects are often destroyed.
(5) The movement of objects fails to follow a "normal" trajectory. The objects behave as if transported, sometimes even following the contours of the furniture.
(6) In rare cases, foreign objects enter closed rooms. When picked up by observers, they are warm to the touch. Objects appear to form in the air.

These, and similar reports, have been part of parapsychological research for hundreds of years.

How can such phenomena be examined? The typical methods used in researching apparitions include questioning those directly affected and other witnesses, the most objective possible documentation of the questionable phenomena (while considering attempts at fraud and manipulation), and finally recording the psychological and social dynamics of the overall situation in which the phenomena occur (Bauer & Lucadou, 1989; Roll, 1976). When attempts are made to film or photograph these phenomena, experience shows that they remain elusive.

In anthropomorphic terms, the apparition gives the impression of being directed by an impish, infantile, or mischievous intelligence; it plays hoaxes, teases us, seems to evade targeted observation, and always occurs wherever one happens not to be looking. The apparition appears to have the intelligence needed to direct events, behaving like a kobold or mischievous spirit, hence the name "poltergeist," meaning "noisy spirit"—a term we have simply adopted in English.

The phenomenon is usually triggered by a particular person, generally adolescent or a little older, or the social group (family) in which they live. Another famous case in Germany examined by Professor Bender was the Rosenheim apparition of 1967/68: the IGPP was called in following a series of physically "inexplicable" phenomena in a lawyer's office in Rosenheim. They included bangs, disruptions to the electrical

The 1723 textbook *Wie man Gespenster und Gespenster-Geschichte prüfen soll*
(How to examine tales of ghosts) reports on the activities of a kobold in a rectory.

circuits and telephones, and objects moving. It turned out that a nineteen-year-old office employee was the likely "focus person." Together with the municipality of Rosenheim and two physicists from Munich, it was possible to document the "anomalous" phenomena so thoroughly that Bender regarded this case as providing evidence for the existence of spontaneous psychokinesis, or "spookery."

The psychodynamic interpretation of the person-related spook is that the apparitions result from the inability to express the tensions, conflicts, or development stages pertaining to the person in question in a "normal" manner, and consequently, they are projected externally. "Ghosts" or "the dead" are assumed to be the origins of these phenomena. According to this interpretation, the focus person's "externalized" problems would find "objective" form, although there is no explanation of why. Ghostly apparitions create a whole consisting of two corresponding halves: one material (physical) and the other mental (psychological). The two halves are mutually dependent, and symbolically entangled. In 1952, psychiatrist C. G. Jung and physicist Wolfgang Pauli introduced the underlying double-aspect theory (*Unus-Mundus*) of the mental and physical to discussions of the paranormal as a principle of synchronicity.

This is regarded as a precursor to "non-local entanglement correlations" in which mental and physical circumstances are understood as equally important epistemic manifestations of a psychophysically neutral and unified reality and has played a key role in developing today's theories of psychophysical correlations.

It has yet to be seen whether the complementary global and local observables, including everyday aspects such as "bonds" versus "autonomy" (which can be seen in cases of apparitions), which are needed for non-local entanglement correlations may be present.

The goal of advising those experiencing apparitions is to decode the meaning or significance of such manifestations in the light of current biographical or family situations. Experience shows that phantoms disappear when the "true" problem is recognized—the phantom is no longer needed and is eventually forgotten. Today, research into such phenomena is on the agenda of the international parapsychological community: historical, sociological, clinical and psychological, experimental, and methodological aspects of phantoms are regularly presented at symposia hosted by organizations such as the Parapsychological Association and the Society for Psychical Research. Furthermore, it can be assumed that phantom appearances will continue to be treated as the most remarkable psychosocial anomalies which mobilize human wishes and fantasies, fears, and defence mechanisms, and will therefore remain an inexhaustible source of inspiration for popular culture in the mass media.

Eberhard Bauer
Research Coordinator
Institute for Frontier Areas of Psychology and Mental Health (IGPP)
Wilhelmstraße 3 A, 79098 Freiburg im Breisgau

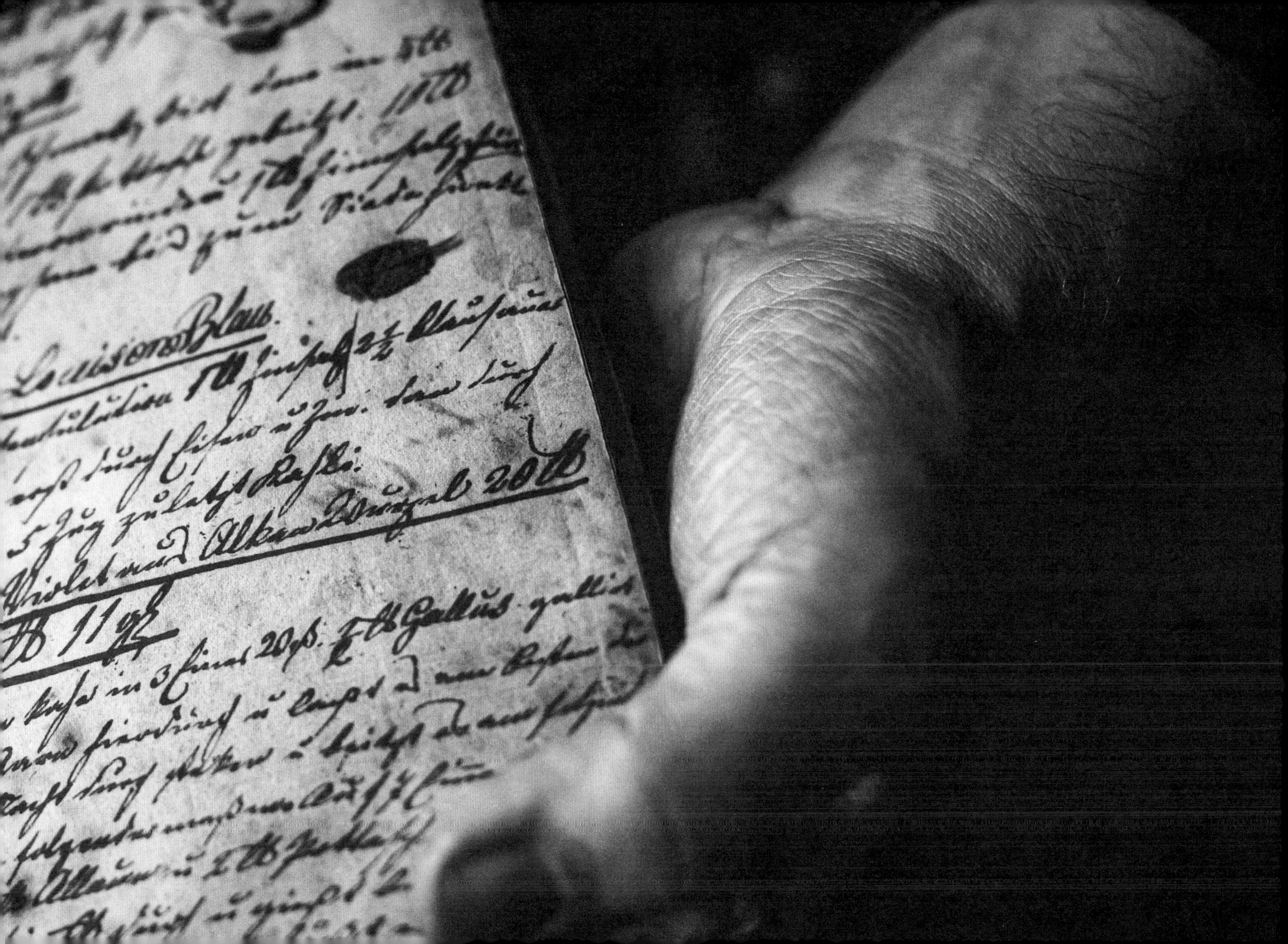

Chapter 4:

In the Mythatelier—
A Glimpse Behind the Scenes

New life is breathed into dusty old tales in Florian Schäfer's "mythatelier." It is here that the large and small creatures of legends and folklore emerge through the craftsman's meticulous skills—including the household spirits in this book. What are the materials and creative processes used to produce these sculptures?

RESEARCH
The design of each figure is always based on extensive research into the historical sources. Whether collections of nineteenth-century legends, records of witchcraft trials, or medieval texts, every effort is made to first understand the beliefs of our ancestors. And always with a critical look at the spirit of those past times, and the historical circumstances which accompanied belief in these beings.

DESIGN
What is often a very diverse range of information is used to draw up an artistic vision of the legendary figure. Size, appearance, hair, and clothing must all be determined, as well as whether the figure should be flexible or adopt a fixed posture.

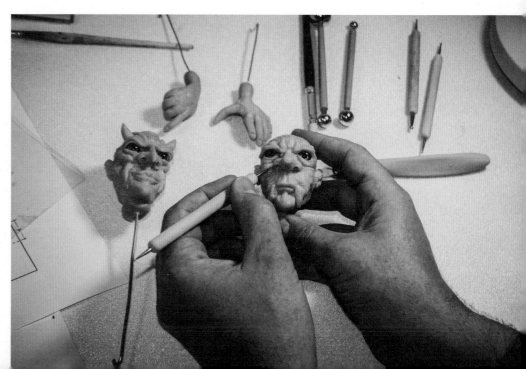

MODELLING

The first step is to build a frame made from stiff wire. This forms the basis for the body and serves to anchor the polymer clay which is applied in several stages and shaped using various tools. Glass eyes lend the figures a particular depth and additional character. Once completed, the individual body parts are cured in a kiln.

PAINTING

The completed figure is then painted with quality acrylic paints. Many thinly applied layers of low viscosity paint lend depth to the features and texture of the skin.

CLOTHING DESIGN

When the body of the figure is completed, the original sketches are used to design a pattern for the clothes. Emphasis is placed on appropriately referencing the underlying story of the legendary figure.

SEWING, STITCHING, EQUIPPING

Wherever possible, natural materials in wool, linen, or at least cotton, are chosen for the clothes. Textiles with an interesting woven pattern can be used to impressive effect. Embroidery and bead decoration further enhance the items of clothing.

FINISHING

The final details are then added: hair, effects of water, or specks of saliva, are attached with special tools. The clothing is "weathered" to give it the typical used look of worn cloth. These elements lend the figures authenticity and character.

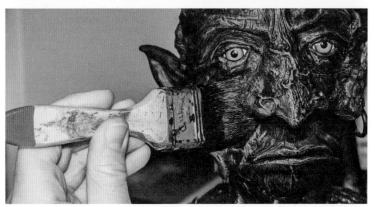

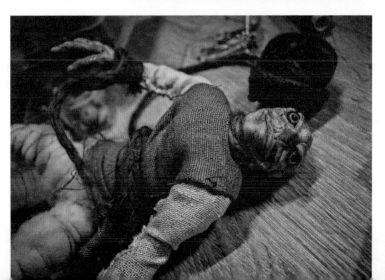

SETTING THE SCENE

After completion, each figure is placed in a scene appropriate to its origins. Photographs for the book were taken in the Freilichtmuseum Hessenpark, the Museumshafen Oevelgönne and the city museum of Camburg. Most were taken by our designer and photographer, Hannah Gritsch, who understands how to capture the wild, legendary nature of our creatures in visual imagery.

ANIMAL FORMS

Taxidermist Tina Tüpke is the creator of our spirits in animal form. This required her to develop her own specific procedures, combining traditional taxidermy techniques with electrotechnics, and in doing so redefining the nature of her craft. Since 2019, she has worked for the company Tierpräparation Waltrop where she creates new memorabilia and miscellaneous decorations on a daily basis, inspired by both the natural world and her own creativity.

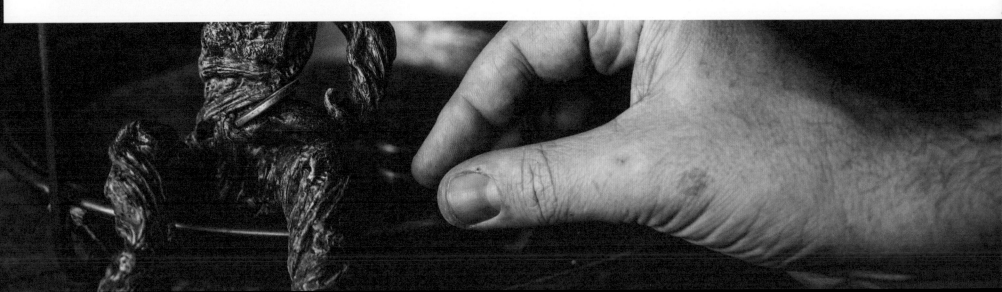

Contrary to the widely held view, taxidermy is more than simply "padding" bodies. Her job involves mould design, casting, modelling, carving, and painting. She also draws on her extensive knowledge of chemical processes and anatomy, as well as behavioural biology. Without a deep interest in the natural world and its fauna, it would be impossible to breathe life into mere shapeless exteriors.

The project needed black animals, but as only a red-gold hen and white rats were available, hair colouring and much experimentation were the order of the day. The first step was to peel off and clean the skins while making as few holes as possible, and then treating it with chemicals. The most time-consuming part of taxidermy is the process of constructing an artificial body which involves the use of a whole range of materials. As well as dual-component PU foam and silicon, traditional wood shavings can also be used which, when applied correctly, can form details such as the muscles.

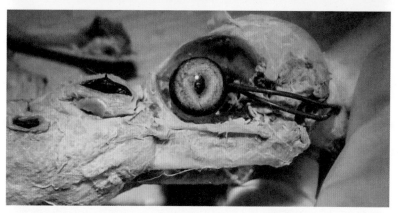

The *Household Spirits* project also used LEDs and circuit boards which have very rarely been used in taxidermy. The wiring under the skin this required involved much experimentation and testing, but finally resulted in magnificent lighting effects.Once the prepared skin has been drawn over the artificial body, the next step is modelling and arranging the external details. Artistic talent is indispensable in creating the gaze, expression, and posture to a degree of precision which gives the animal its realistic appearance. The taxidermist must constantly check the work for at least two weeks after the animal has been finished, to correct any changes that emerge during the drying period. When the animal has been cured it is then coloured, using both an airbrush and a traditional paintbrush.

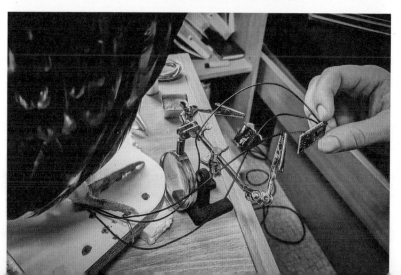

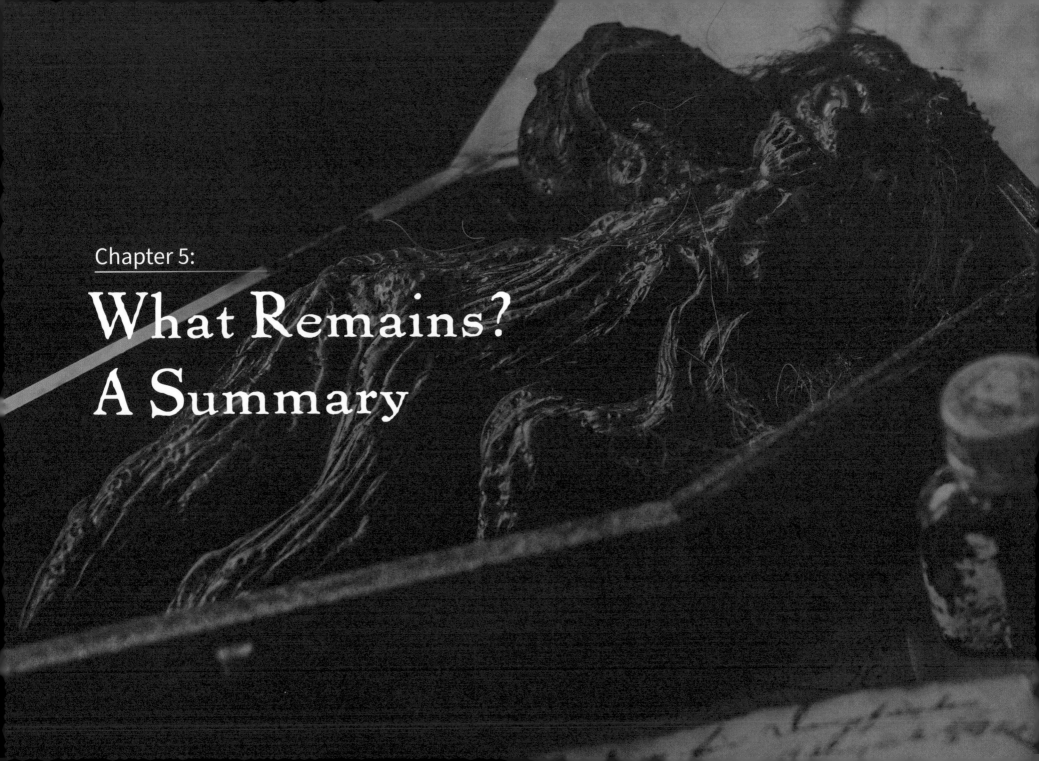

Chapter 5:

What Remains?
A Summary

"In the end, these tales only prove that supernatural events are part of human nat-ure, revealing a side which is simultaneously dreadful, yet enticing."

From Petzoldt, Leander (1989): *Dämonenfurcht und Gottvertrauen.*
Zur Geschichte und Erforschung unserer Volkssagen, Darmstadt, p. 167.

Visiting old farmhouses and reconstructions of former longhouses today, we may sense something of the awe which people of ancient times once felt in the darkness. In a world in which the shadows of the night were not yet banished by electricity, the gloomy spaces in the house appeared far more mystical and dangerous, the dark timber frames threatening, with the warming glow of the hearth blinding observers to the goings-on in the furthest corners.

Together we have explored the spirits of the house. We went far back in time and have certainly had a few unexpected encounters. We examined not only the house-hold spirits of the title, but also the sociocultural and political backgrounds to the

beliefs in these beings. The departure of the wichtel and fortunes brought by the alraun have a far greater meaning than the actual stories. Whenever we look at tales of household spirits, they reveal to us something of those who told them. They can be understood as a symbolic expression of the existing norms, values, and ideas about the environment, work, and social relationships in each of their social settings. Transposing one's own culture and social principles to the natural world—as is clearly demonstrated in the descriptions of dwarfs—creates an opportunity to evaluate and process sociocultural developments.

In a 1961 congress paper on the function of folktales, the medieval historian Kurt Schier (*1929) outlined six fundamental needs which he regarded as the spiritual motives behind folktales and legends:

(1)   The need to explain the world;
(2)   To mythologize and demonize it;

(3)   To focus on specific manifestations of general occurrences;
(4)   Create a heroic figure that can lead to hero worship;
(5)   The need for a higher order; and
(6)   Negation of that order.

The legends arise from the urge to narrate, in turn based on the need to explain and mythologize. The folklorist Leander Petzoldt also notes that popular legends were "socially critical," but rather than actively criticizing society, they took on an ideological function in an attempt to maintain the traditional order.

"Every third farmer had a kobold in the house; the supernatural was feared in every corner. Devils pushed and forced themselves through the walls at night, first an eye would break through, then a tongue: only prayer held the entire demon back. Spirits lived in the woods, wild and gentle, headless men at crossroads, little moss women hunted by Satan. Even in the towns there were spirits of the night, often curious types, in Frankfurt the horse in chains, in Worms the fiery owl."

Ernst Bloch. "Technik und Geistererscheinungen," in *Literarische Aufsätze* (Gesamtausabe. Vol. 9), Frankfurt, 1935.

Motives such as the violation of taboos, punishment, and human conflicts over property are all common in legends about household spirits. Here legends demonstrate their social function, and reflect rural attitudes to life, with a mixture of work and religious obligations. The legends mirror the farmers' strongly traditional lifestyles and dependence on the natural world, as well as existing power relations. But, Petzoldt concludes, as the subjects of these tales failed to recognize these dependencies, and rationality had no place, they would adopt a mythological view of the world, with powers determining human fates. So were the contents of legends ever actually believed?

Archaeological sources indicate that active belief in household spirits had its origins in the medieval period, while later nineteenth-century collections of legends sketch out past beliefs. There is insufficient historical evidence to determine the extent to which the medieval kobold corresponds to its twentieth-century counterpart. If, and when, there was a transition from an active to a redundant belief in household spirits is difficult to quantify. The available sources suggest this may have occurred at some time during the seventeenth to eighteenth centuries. Trial records and legal queries reporting on practised beliefs do not necessarily describe true popular beliefs, although it cannot be ruled out that subsequent generations, engaged in nostalgic reverie, integrated these ideas into their own narratives.

"Where is the will-o'-the-wisp behind the car headlights racing down a country road; how can the death-watch be heard when the farmer tunes his radio to London? The klabautermann is homeless now that the sailing ships are gone; a Kobold behind a gas oven or the central heating is not spooky, but ridiculous and tasteless."

Bloch, Ernst. "Technik und Geistererscheinungen." *Literarische Aufsätze*, Gesamtausgabe. Vol. 9, (Frankfurt: 1935), p. 358–365.

The idea that the belief in ghosts fell victim to the Enlightenment and industrialization is an attractive one. However, Bloch overlooks the human psyche, itself as dark as the corner of old timbered houses. It should be noted that a certain percentage of the population continues to believe in various supernatural phenomena, including poltergeists and ghostly apparitions, through to the present day. Constantly shifting popular belief and irrational views of the world are still observable today, even though it may not always be ghosts whose appearances people believe they see in everyday life: the idea of numinous beings such as natural spirits and protective angels is hugely popular in today's neo-pagan and esoteric circles. In online forums, such as those presented by Simone Stiefbold in her dissertation on changelings, users today ask how they can protect their child from being exchanged. This is reminiscent of Lutz Röhrich and other beings:

"Of longest duration is the witch: in many places people still believe in witches. Equally, the original beliefs in the legends of the dead are usually retained through to the present day."

Lutz Röhrich, *Märchen und Wirklichkeit*, (Wiesbaden: 1964) p. 11.

There is a similar level of interest in household spirits. The question "How do I recognize if I have a household spirit?" was posed on the German *Allmystery* online forum in 2016, with various aspects of these beings subsequently discussed. While some users offered joking replies, several "experts" joined in, with reports of their own experiences or hearsay.

Modern fantasy literature, much of it based on a mythological past but usually with significantly new interpretations, also appears to be incorporated into esoteric beliefs, adopting either traditional or modern narratives. Major artists such as Arthur Rackham, John Bauer, and Brian Froud have also had a significant impact, shaping our images of fairies, trolls, and kobolds since the nineteenth century.

Here the contamination which has already proved an obstacle in the literary analysis of old textual sources is pushed to the extreme. Modern linguistic parlance conflates kobolds, wichtel, dwarfs, and gnomes, sometimes treating them synonymously, altering them at will, and recreating them. It is fascinating to see how the educational role of spirit beings remains to the present day. Stories of ghosts are not usually believed by those telling them, and children increasingly reflect on their content as they grow up.

Narratives shift as society changes, and this seems particularly applicable to household spirits. In the modern day, we see household spirits as bogeymen, metaphors, or modern figures used for advertising purposes. The often-extreme dissociation from their original context, and massive reinterpretation, especially in fantastic and esoteric literature, are typical narrative developments.

In a "fact-free" world, the actual history no longer appears to play a role. Any author can invent their own "kobold" for their own purposes. History is not a cogent argument for a current narrative; a diffuse "perceived past" is sufficient. It would therefore seem to be all the more important that this book highlights the historical and cultural backgrounds of household spirits in German folklore. Hopefully, the popularity of these fantastic motifs can be used to discover our cultural history in a new and fresh manner. When we see the fantastic in our daily encounters, we will perhaps go through life more mindfully and with greater enthusiasm.

This was the aim behind the extensive research into the beings you have met in this book. Our journey into the dark corners of our houses has thus come to its (temporary) conclusion. The spirits in the house have more to offer than simply amusement and the chance to send shivers down our spines. They offer an insight into the psyche of our ancestors as they managed their fears and desires, in their public and private lives.

Your Household Spirit Hunters

Bibliography

BIBLIOGRAPHY AND IMAGE SOURCES

GENERAL:

Adelung, Johann Christoph. *Grammatisch-kritisches Wörterbuch der Hochdeutschen Mundart.* Vienna: 1811.

Agricola, Johannes. *Das ander teyl gemainer Tewtscher Sprichwörter, mit ihrer außlegung hat fünffthalb hundert newer Wörtter.* Nuremberg: 1529.

Arrowsmith, Nancy. *Die Welt der Naturgeister. Handbuch zur Bestimmung der Wald-, Feld-, Wasser-, Haus-, Berg-, Hügel-, und Luftgeister aller europäischen Länder.* Frankfurt: Goldmann, 1984.

Baader, Bernhard. *Volkssagen aus dem Lande Baden und den angrenzenden Gegenden.* Vol. 1. Karlsruhe: 1851.

Bächtold-Stäubli, Hanns et al. *Handwörterbuch des deutschen Aberglaubens.* Berlin/Leipzig: Walter de Gruyter, 1927.

Barkley, Julie, and Nannette Lewis, eds. "Folk-Lore and Legends." The Project Gutenberg eBook of Folk-lore and Legends: Germany, by Anonymous. Edinburgh University Press, December 11, 2008. https://gutenberg.org/files/27499/27499-h/27499-h.htm#Page_136.

Bartsch, Karl. *Sagen, Märchen und Gebräuche aus Meklenburg 1–2.* Vienna: 1879.

Bechstein, Ludwig. *Deutsches Sagenbuch,* trans. Georg Wigand. Leipzig: 1853.

Bechstein, Ludwig. *Thüringer Sagenbuch.* Vienna & Leipzig: C. A. Hartlebens, 1858.

Beck, Martin. *Eine Zauberwurzel. Kulturgeschichtliche Skizze.* Leipzig: Die Gartenlaube, 1893.

Beitl, Richard. *Wörterbuch der deutschen Volkskunde.* 3rd edition. Stuttgart: Kröner, 1974.

"Bible Gateway Passage: Genesis 30—New International Version." Bible Gateway. Harper Collins Christian Publishing. Accessed May 22, 2022. https://www.biblegateway.com/passage/?search=Genesis+2&version=NIV.

Bloch, Ernst. "Technik und Geistererscheinungen" *Literarische Aufsätze,* Gesamtausabe. Vol. 9. Frankfurt: 1935/62, p. 358-365.

Bräuner, Johann Jacob. *Physicalisch-und Historisch-Erörterte Curiositaeten.* Frankfurt: 1737.

Charlemagne. *Capitulatio de partibus Saxione.* (p. 782).

Delrio, Martin Anton. *Disquisitionum magicarum,* Part 1. Louvain: G. Rivius, 1599.

Depiny, Dr. Albert. *Oberösterreichisches Sagenbuch.* Linz: 1932.

Dietz, Josef. *Aus der Sagenwelt des Bonner Landes.* Röhrscheid: 1965.

Eisel, Robert. *Sagenbuch des Voigtlandes.* Gera: Rockstuhl, 1871.

Erich, Oswald A. & Beitl, Richard. *Wörterbuch der deutschen Volkskunde.* Leipzig: Kröner, 1936.

Frahm, Ludwig. *Norddeutsche Sagen von Schleswig-Holstein bis zum Harz.* A. C. Reher, 1890.

Grässe, Johann Georg Theodor. *Sagenbuch des Preußischen Staates 1–2.* Glogau, 1868/71.

Grimm, Jacob. *Deutsche Mythologie.* Reprint of the 4th edition (1875 – 78). Wiesbaden: Drei Lilien publishing house, 1992.

Grimm, Jacob & Wilhelm. *Deutsche Sagen.* Munich: 1965.

Grohmann, Josef Virgil. *Sagen-Buch von Böhmen und Mähren. 1: Sagen aus Böhmen.* Calbe: Prag, 1863.

Heine, Heinrich. *Romanzero, Book Two, Lamentations.* Hamburg: 1851.

Heine, Heinrich. *Werke und Briefe in zehn Bänden.* Vol. 1. Berlin and Weimar: 1972.

Heinz, G. *Die Sage vom Oberfränkischen Holzfräulein.* Frankenwald: 1926, p. 15–16.

Hupfauf, Erich. *Hifalan Und Hafalan Sagen Aus Dem Zillertal.* Schwaz: Berenkamp, 1995.

Jahn, Ulrich. *Volkssagen aus Pommern und Rügen.* Berlin: Mayer & Müller, 1889.

Jolles, André. *Einfache Formen. Legende, Sage, Mythe, Rätsel, Spruch, Kasus, Memorabile, Märchen, Witz.* Second unrevised edition. Darmstadt: Wissenschaftliche Buchgesellschaft, 1958.

Keightley, Thomas. *The Fairy Mythology.* Vol. II. London: Whittaker, Treachers, and Co., 1833.

"Kobold." Duden, German online dictionary. Accessed May 16, 2022. https://www.duden.de/suchen/dudenonline/kobold.

Kuhn, Adalbert. *Märkische Sagen und Märchen nebst einem Anhange von Gebräuchen und Aberglauben.* Berlin: 1843.

Kühn, Dietrich. *Sagen und Legenden aus Thüringen.* Weimar: Wartburg, 1989.

Lindig, Erika. *Hausgeister. Die Vorstellungen übernatürlicher Schützer und Helfer in der deutschen Sagenüberlieferung,* Artes populares. Lausanne: Peter Lang GmbH, Internationaler Verlag der Wissenschaften, 1987.

Linhart, Dagmar. *Hausgeister in Franken.* Dettelbach: Röll, 1995.

Löber, Karl. *Haigerer Heft. Beitrage zur Geschichte und zum Leben der Stadt Haiger und ihres Raumes. Heft II. Sagen/Vogeschichte.* Stadt Haiger: Stadtverwaltung Haiger, 1972.

Löhr, Johann Andreas Christian. *Das Buch der Maehrchen für Kindheit und Jugend, nebst etzlichen Schnaken und Schnurren, anmutig und lehrhaftig.* Vol. 1. Leipzig: 1819.

Luther, Dr. Martin. *Sämtliche Werke.* Vol. 60-62, (Digitized: Harvard University, 2008), original 1854. https://books.google.ca/books?id=_jMoAAAAYAAJ&dq=martin+luther+on+%22wichtlin%22&source=gbs_navlinks_s.

Mannhardt, Wilhelm & Heuschkel, Walter. *Wald- und Feldkulte.* Berlin: Borntraeger, 1875.

Müller, Josef. *Sagen aus Uri 1–3.* Vol. 1. Basel: 1926.

Panzer, Friedrich. *Bayerische Sagen und Bräuche.* Munich: Kaiser, 1855.

Petzoldt, Leander. *Dämonenfurcht und Gottvertrauen.* Darmstadt: Wissenschaftliche Buchgesellschaft, 1989.

Petzoldt, Leander. *Kleines Lexikon der Dämonen und der Elementargeister.* 2nd revised edition. Munich: C.H. Beck'sche Verlagsbuchhandlung, 1995.

Petzoldt, Leander. *Deutsche Volkssagen.* Wiesbaden: Marix, 2007.

Peuckert, Will-Erich. *Deutscher Volksglaube des Spätmittelalters.* Stuttgart: W. Spemann Verlag, 1942.

Praetorius, Johannes. *Anthropodemus plutonicus. Das ist eine neue Weltbeschreibung,* p. 1–2, Magdeburg, 1666/67.

Ranke, Friedrich. *Volkssagenforschung. Vorträge und Aufsätze.* Breslau: Maruschke & Berendt, 1935.

Ranke, Kurt et al. *Enzyklopädie des Märchens. Handwörterbuch zur historischen und vergleichenden Erzählforschung.* Berlin: Walter de Gruyter, 1975ff.

Reichhard, Elias Caspar. *Vermischte Beiträge einer nähern Einsicht in das gesammte Geisterreich.* Helmstedt: 1781.

Röhrich, Lutz. *Märchen und Wirklichkeit.* Wiesbaden: Franz Steiner, 1964.

Röhrich, Lutz. "Was soll und kann die Sagenforschung leisten? Einige aktuelle Probleme unseres Faches." In: *Röhrich, Lutz [Ed.]: Probleme der Sagenforschung.* Freiburg im Breisgau: Deutsche Forschungsgemeinschaft, 1973, p. 13–34.

Röhrich, Roland. *Franz Xaver Schönwerth: Leben und Werk.* Lassleben: 1975.

Schambach, Georg & Müller, Wilhelm. *Niedersächsische Sagen und Märchen—Aus dem Munde des Volkes gesammelt und mit Anmerkungen und Abhandlungen.* Göttingen: Vandenhoeck & Ruprecht, 1955.

Schell, Otto. *Bergische Sagen.* Second extended edition. Elberfeld: Martini & Grüttefien, 1922.

Schöppner, Alexander. *Sagenbuch der bayerischen Lande.* Munich: Rieger, 1866.

Schönwerth, Franz. *Aus der Oberpfalz. Sitten und Sagen 1–3,* Augsburg.

Schöppner, Alexander. *Sagenbuch der bayerischen Lande,* Rieger, München.

Schönwerth, Franz. *Aus der Oberpfalz. Sitten und Sagen 1–3.* Vol. 2. Augsburg: 1857/58/59.

Schulze, Ursula & Grosse, Siegfried. *Das Nibelungenlied.* Ditzingen: Reclam, Philipp, jun. GmbH, 2011.

Spiegel, Karl. *Die bayerischen Sagen vom Kobold, Bayerische Hefte für Volkskunde,* München.

von Zimmern, Froben Christoph. *Zimmerische Chronik.* Vol. III. Verein, Stuttgart: Karl August Barack, Litterar, 1881.

Simek, Rudolf. *Lexikon der germanischen Mythologie.* Stuttgart: Alfred Kröner, 1995.

von Hohenheim, Theophrast & Pörksen, Gunhild. *Das Buch von den Nymphen, Sylphen, Pygmaeen, Salamandern und übrigen Geistern Faksimile der Ausgabe Basel 1590. In der Übertragung und mit einem Nachwort von Gunhild Pörksen.* Rangsdorf: Basilisken-Presse im Verlag Natur & Text, 2003.

Wenig, Ernst Karl. *Thüringer Sagen.* Rudolstadt: Greifenverlag, 1992.

Widmann, Enoch. *Chronik der Stadt Hof.* Wurzburg: Wissenschaftlicher Kommissionsverlag, 2015.

Wucke, Christian Ludwig. *Sagen der mittleren Werra.* Vol. 2. Norderstedt: Hansebooks, 1864.

Zaunert, Paul. *Westfälische Sagen.* Jena: Diederichs Verlag, 1927.

Zaunert, Paul (1969): *Rheinland Sagen.* Vol. 1. Jena: Diederichs Verlag, 1969.

Zimmern, Froben Christoph. *Zimmern Chronicle.* Vol. 3. Freiburg: 1881.

SPECIALIST CONTRIBUTIONS

TOBIAS JANOUSCHEK: OF *LARES* AND *PENATES*—HONOURING HOUSEHOLD DEITIES IN THE ROMAN EMPIRE

LITERATURE:

Wiegels, Rainer. "*Religio Celtica!—Einige Überlegungen zur Götterverehrung im gallisch-germanischen Provinzgebiete.*" In: K. Matijević (Ed.), *Kelto-Römische Gottheiten und ihre Verehrer.* Trier: 2014, 9–40.

Behrens, Gustav. *Germanische und gallische Götter in römischem Gewand.* Mainz: 1944.

Simon, Erika. *Die Götter der Römer.* Mainz: 1990.

Roscher, Wilhelm Heinrich (Ed.). *Ausführliches Lexikon der Griechischen und Römischen Mythologie.* Leipzig: 1894.

IMAGES:

Image on page 158: Roman statue in bronze
Exhibited in the British Museum, 1st to 3rd century AD.
Creative Commons Attribution 4.0 International Licence, Photo: www.britishmuseum.org

Image on page 159: "Casa dei Vettii – Larario"
Photographed by: Patricio Lorente
(https://commons.wikimedia.org/wiki/File:Casa_dei_Vettii_-_Larario.jpg)
Licence: https://creativecommons.org/licenses/by-sa/2.5/legalcode

PROFESSOR TOBIAS GÄRTNER: TEXTUAL AND ARCHAEOLOGICAL SOURCES FOR BELIEFS IN HOUSEHOLD SPIRITS IN THE MEDIEVAL PERIOD

LITERATURE:

Capelle, Torsten. *Eisenzeitliche Bauopfer.* Frühmittelalterliche Studien 21, Berlin: de Gruyter, 1987, p. 182–205.

Fehring, Günter P. *Stadtarchäologie in Deutschland.* Stuttgart: Archäologie in Deutschland, Sonderheft, 1996.

Gärtner, Tobias. *Hausgeister im Mittelalter.* Schriftliche Überlieferung und archäologische Funde.

Mitteilungen der Berliner Gesellschaft für Anthropologie. Ethnologie und Urgeschichte 26, Leidorf: Rahden/Westf, 2005, p. 19–28.

Gärtner, Tobias. *Zur Interpretation mittelalterlicher Bauopfer aus Hannover.* Nachrichten aus Niedersachsens Urgeschichte 74, Stuttgart: Theiss, 2005, p. 195–208.

Kantonales Museum für Urgeschichte(n) Zug (Ed.) *Merkur & Co. Kult und Religion im römischen Haus.* Kantonales Museum für Urgeschichte(n), 2010.

Klapper, Josef. "Deutscher Volksglaube in ältester Zeit." In: *Communications of the Silesian Society for Folklore.* Vol. 17. Breslau: Marcus, 1915, p. 19–57.

Lecouteux, Claude. *Eine Welt im Abseits. Zur niederen Mythologie und Glaubenswelt des Mittelalters.* Dettelbach: J.H. Röll Verlag, 2000.

Scholkmann, Barbara. "Medieval pottery finds from Saulgau, district of Sigmaringen." In: *Research and reports on medieval archeology in Baden-Württemberg.* Vol. 7. Stuttgart, 1981, p. 421–434.

IMAGES:

Image on page 161: Building sacrifice of dog and ceramic pot, circa 1300 (Leipzig, Preussergässchen: Fehring, 1996).

Image on page 162: Saulgau, Schützenstrasse 7, ceramic pot with incised cross potent from a cellar wall (after Scholkmann 1981).

PROFESSOR RUDOLF SIMEK: LARGE TROLLS, SMALL TROLLS, HOUSEHOLD SPIRITS

LITERATURE:

Simek, Rudolf. *Trolle: ihre Geschichte von der nordischen Mythologie bis zum.* (Köln/Weimar/Vienna 2018: Böhlau Verlag, 2018).

Bengt af Klintberg. *Svenska Folksägner.* Stockholm: 1986.

IMAGES:

Both wood engravings (page 165) from **Magnus, Olaus (1557)**: *Historia de gentibus Septentrionalibus.* Book 3.

BURKHARD KLING: *DIE IRISCHEN ELFENMÄRCHEN* OF THE BROTHERS GRIMM

LITERATURE:

Briggs, Katharine Mary. *An Encyclopedia of Fairies, Hobgoblins, Brownies, Boogies, and Other Supernatural Creatures.* New York: Pantheon Books, 1976.

Grimm, Jacob. *Deutsche Mythologie.* 1st edition. Göttingen: Dieterich, 1835.

Grimm, Jacob and Grimm, Wilhelm. *Kinder- und Hausmärchen.* Berlin: Realschulbuchhandlung, 1812.

Grimm, Jacob and Grimm, Wilhelm. *Irische Elfenmärchen.* Leipzig: 1826.

Grimm, Jacob and Grimm, Wilhelm. "Irische Elfenmärchen." In: *der Übertragung der Brüder Grimm.* Frankfurt & Leipzig: 1987.

Koch, John T. *Celtic culture: a historical encyclopedia.* Vol. 1–5. Santa Barbara: ABC-Clio, 2006.

Martus, Steffen. *Die Brüder Grimm.* Eine Biographie, Berlin: Rowholt, 2009.

O'Donnell, Elliott. *The Banshee.* London/Edinburgh: Sands & Co., 1923.

Petzoldt, Leander. *Kleines Lexikon der Dämonen und Elementargeister.* Munich: Beck, 1990.

Rölleke, Heinz. *Grimms Märchen und ihre Quellen.* Die literarischen Vorlagen der Grimmschen Märchen synoptisch vorgestellt und kommentiert. 2nd edition. Trier: Wissenschaftlicher Verlag, 2004.

Rölleke, Heinz. *Alt wie der Wald.* Reden und Aufsätze zu den Märchen der Brüder Grimm, Wissenschaftlicher Verlag: Trier, 2006.

Scheede, Hans Georg. *Die Brüder Grimm.* Hanau: Cocon-Verlag, 2009.

"Thomas Crofton Croker," *Encyclopædia Britannica.* 11th edition. *Constantine Pavlovich to Demidov.* Vol. 7. Horace Everett Hooper: United States, 1911, p. 482.

William Butler Yeats. *Fairy and folk tales of Ireland.* Gerrards Cross: Smythe, 1973.

JANIN PISAREK: THE CHANGELING—A FIEND IN THE CRADLE

LITERATURE:

Caesar, Wolfgang. "Wechselbalg—Mehr Als Ein Albtraum." DAZ.online: Aug 2019. Accessed March 2022, https://www.deutsche-apotheker-zeitung.de/daz-az/2013/daz-15-2013/wechselbalg-mehr-als-ein-albtraum.

Piaschewski, Gisela. "Wechselbalg." In: *Handwörterbuch des Deutschen Aberglaubens.* Vol. 9, Ed. E. Hoffmann-Krayer and Hanns Bächtold-Stäubli, Berlin: Walter de Gruyter, 1938, p. 835–864.

Stiefbold, Simone. "Mit dem Wechselbalg denken. Menschen und Nicht-Menschen." In: *lebensweltlichen Narrativen.* Marburg: Jonas Verlag, 2015.

Stiefbold, Simone. "Vom ‚Anderen' zum ‚Anderssein'? Der Wechselbalg in Saaski aus dem Moor." In: *Institut für Sozialanthropologie und Empirische Kulturwissenschaft (ISEK).* Zürich: Universität Zürich kids+media, 2015, p. 20–37.

IMAGES:

Image on page 170: Child with hydrocephalus: Illustration by Michael Schmerbach in Rudolph Virchow. Gesammelte Abhandlungen zur wissenschaftlichen Medicin, Frankfurt, 1856, p. 953.

Image on page 171: A mother discovers the changeling. "The Changeling" by Henry Fuseli, Kunsthaus Zürich, 1780.

Image on page 172: The Devil steals a child and replaces it with a changeling. Excerpt from The Legend of St. Stephen, painting by Martino di Bartolomeo (early fifteenth century).

Image on page 173: Child with genetic hydrocephalus (also called water on the brain, or dropsy).

Photographed in Sheffield, Herman Bernard (1871): Modern diagnosis and treatment of diseases of children; a treatise on the medical and surgical diseases of infancy and childhood.

EBERHARD BAUER: SPOOKS AND GHOSTLY APPARITIONS OF THE PAST AND PRESENT

LITERATURE:

Bauer, Eberhard. "Exkursionen in »Nachtgebiete der Natur«—Justinus Kerner und die historische Spukforschung." In: *Zeitschrift für Parapsychologie und Grenzgebiete der Psychologie.* Vol. 31. Frieburg: Institut fur Grenzgebiete der Psychologie, 1989, p. 3–19.

Bauer, Eberhard & Lucadou, Walter v. (Ed.) (1989): *Zeitschrift für Parapsychologie und Grenzgebiete der Psychologie.* Freiburg: Universitätsbibliothek, 2012. Accessed March 2022, http://dl.ub.uni-freiburg.de/diglit/zs_parapsychologie_ga.

Bauer, Eberhard & Schetsche, Michael (Ed.). *Alltägliche Wunder—Erfahrungen mit dem Übersinnlichen.* Würzburg: Ergon, 2003.

Bender, Hans. "Neue Entwicklungen in der Spukforschung." In: *Zeitschrift für Parapsychologie und Grenzgebiete der Psychologie.* Vol. 12. Frieburg: Instut fur Grenzgebiete der Psychologie, 1970, p. 1–18.

Gauld, Alan & Cornell, Tony. *Poltergeists.* Hove: White Crow Books, 2018.

Moser, Fanny. *Spuk.* Ein Rätsel der Menschheit, Freiburg: Olten Walter, 1977.

Puhle, Annekatrin. Sechs historische Poltergeistfälle aus dem 18. Jahrhundert in Deutschland, in *Zeitschrift für Parapsychologie und Grenzgebiete der Psychologie.* Vol. 41. Frieburg: Instut fur Grenzgebiete der Psychologie, 1999, p. 23–40.

Roll, William G. *Der Poltergeist.* Freiburg: Aurum, 1976.

Willin, Melvyn. *The Enfield Poltergeist Tapes.* Epsom: White Crow Books, 2019.

IMAGES:

Image on page 174: Illustration of apparitions in Cideville, France, 1850–1851. Illustration from Damien, Michel (Ed.) *Les hôtes invisibles: les dossiers noirs des maisons hantées.* Paris: Tchou, 1978, p. 22.

Image on page 175: Poltergeist in the shape of kobold-like beings. Illustration by Hookham, Frontispiece in Price, Harry. *Poltergeist over England.* London: Country Life, 1945.

Image on page 176: The 1723 textbook *Wie man Gespenster und Gespenster-Geschichte prüfen soll* (Lessons on How to Test Ghosts and Ghost Stories) reports on the activities of a kobold in a rectory. Heinish, Jeremiah. *Wie man Gespenster und Gespenster-Geschichte prüfen soll.* Germany: SLUB Dresden, 1723. Accessed March 2022, https://digital.slub-dresden.de/en/workview/dlf/16654/5.

IMAGE CREDITS:

Credits for the historical image materials are included in the caption under each image.
The publisher and editor have made every effort to identify all copyright holders.
Where we have not succeeded in doing so, please contact us.

Page 89: Photograph reproduced with the kind permission of the Archäologische Freilichtmuseum Oerlinghausen.

Acknowledgements

Managing a project such as this requires not only time, but also the help and support of many people. We would therefore like to offer our heartfelt thanks all those who have contributed to making this project a success:

We thank the following museums who made their premises available for the photography in this book:

- **The Freilichtmuseum Hessenpark** (Petra Naumann, Carsten Sobik and Iris von Stephanitz)
- **The Stadtmuseum Camburg** (Pauline Lörzer)
- Benjamin Schäfer, **Deutsche Märchenstraße e.V.** for a wide range of support
- Gudrun Bartels, **Göttinger Märchenland e.V.** for important contacts
- **The Archäologische Freilichtmuseum Oerlinghausen** (Dr. Greta Civis) for providing images
- Gefion Apel and Dr. Heinrich Stiewe of the **LWL-Freilichtmuseum Detmold** for expert suggestions and valuable discussions

The authors of the specialist contributions:

- **Tobias Janouschek**
- **Professor Gärtner**
- **Professor Simek**
- **Burkhard Kling**
- **Eberhard Bauer**
- **Janin Pisarek**

Hannah Gritsch for our online presence

We would also like to thank the publisher "Eye of Newt" and especially **Stephanie Dror** for the uncomplicated contact during the translation and preparation of the English edition.

All supporters of the Forgotten Creatures project, in particular its patrons:

- **Timo Weifenbach**
- **Marcel Bauer**
- **Una Halitschke**
- **Marc Reifenberger**
- **Benjamin Zogg**
- **Mike Heinrichs**
- **Christian von Aster**
- **Yannic Bochert**
- **Felix Zimmermann**
- **Anne-Kathrin Gog**
- **Max Schiller**
- **Christine Rauscher**

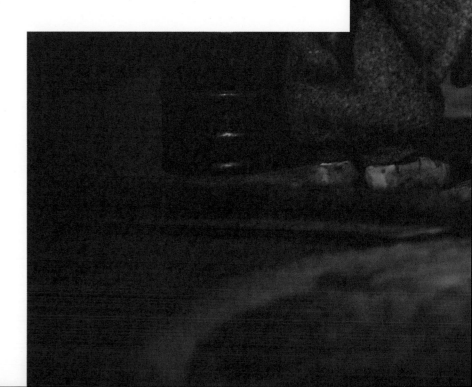

WOOL OF BAT

a book from

EYE of NEWT
BOOKS